Jazzi,
Thank you so much
for supporting me!! :)

The Story to Tell

The Journey to Forgiveness

THE STORY TO TELL

The Journey to Forgiveness

a novel

CI CI LAMAR

C. R. Lamar Enterprises
P.O. Box 18232
Cleveland Heights, Ohio 44118

This book is a work of fiction. Any references to historical events, real people, or real places are used fictitiously. Other names, characters, places, and events are products of the author's imagination, and any resemblance to actual events or places or persons, living or dead, is entirely coincidental.

Manufactured in the United States of America.

Library of Congress Control Number: 2017906674

ISBN: 978-0-69288-399-0

DEDICATION

To my **creator**,

the almighty I thank you for having mercy and patience with me when many times I was undeserving.

To my **mother**,

and from one mother to another, if there were no you there would be no me and for that reason alone you will always have my love and respect.

To my **father**,

you are the very reason I live with a purpose. I witnessed your selfless dedication on countless days (which you referred to as your blood, sweat and tears). And that instilled in me the blessings behind hard work.

To my **brother**,

since the beginning of time you were my #1 fan. Thank you for seeing my worth even when I didn't.

To my **sons,**

I love you more than life. And I will give up mine any given day for you. Don't ever let my love and sacrifice for you go in vain.

*I want to send a special thank you to *all professional parties* who assisted me with making my dream become a reality.

IN LOVING MEMORY OF

My Father

My brothers

My grandparents

My great-grand mother

You are who you think you are.....

-AUTHOR UNKNOWN

There is no greater agony than bearing an untold story inside of you

-MAYA ANGELO

ONE

I DIDN'T HAVE TO GO TO REHAB TO KNOW THAT THE FIRST step to change and or sobriety is admitting you have a problem. I will be the first to admit that it isn't an easy thing to do; to look in the mirror and say, "I messed up"!! However, it is easiest to point fingers and place blame anywhere but self.

So here it goes….

My name is Sahara Ramal and I have a problem. However, I take full responsibility for my life and my actions.

I played every moment I've ever experienced over and over again in my head trying to rationalize cause and effect. Thinking if this one thing or event may have been altered in any way how different my life may have gone. Similar to the movie, "Butterfly Effect". I'm still young and I know I have time but I can't help but to wonder "What if"!

I held on to anger and resentment so long that it began to eat away at my soul. I became unrecognizable to myself.

For forever it seems like I have always had these dreams. Something like an outer body experience. One may call it Deja Vu. Not sure if I believe in that stuff or not. But something is going on and has been going on for some time. Initially, I would think that I've never met a person before, done something or gone to a particular place. But on the other hand, I can recall specific details about the place, person or thing. It's almost like seeing someone and knowing for sure you know them and remembering a conversation you all may have had but not knowing exactly when or where it took place. And you may or may not remember their name.

Or having a dream that you're falling off a cliff and wake up to find that you fell from the bed. Or the bathroom dreams when you feel that you must urinate in your dream and awaken to a warm dribble of urine against your skin and rushing to really reach a commode.

Twenty years earlier...

"Violet you are under arrest. You have the right to remain silent anything you say or do maybe use against you in the court of law. You have the right to an attorney and if you cannot afford one, one will be appointed to you .."

Were the final words I heard from the officer before seeing my mother dragged away in hand cuffs; while I held the hand of the nice Caucasian woman in the tan high end trench coat outside our three bedrooms apartment. I never realized that this very moment would be the defining point of my life!

TWO

IT'S RAINING CATS AND DOGS OUTSIDE. AND I HAVE NO desire whatsoever to go outside but it's my new boo's birthday. I decided to clean his house spotless, cook some dinner, throw on some sexy lingerie and give him the best sex he's ever had (so he tells me) with a little extra "umph"!

In the midst of getting dressed in my pearl white laced corset top with matching thong and white peep toe platform Louboutin pumps, I hear the front door to the house open. I made a dash for the floor to protect my surprise.

Instantly I began to have flashbacks. It was funny like that sometimes, how a smell or an abstract object brought about vivid memories of my past. I lay on the floor of the bedroom looking at all the small things that had managed to make their way beneath the bed and escape our memory without missing them: a few socks, lip gloss, lighter, Kleenex and a rat tail comb.

Watching and waiting for my birthday boy to leave out again, jogged my memory. Dec 1997, I was wakening up startled by the commotion coming from the front door. I was too scared to move or even go see what was going on for that matter. I laid in bed still as a tree and I hid beneath the cover.

I hoped that whoever had come in our home wouldn't think I was there had they come and looked. I also thought to hide beneath the bed but I was scared that if I moved the springs in the mattress would screech or worst I would trip over one of the many objects that lied on the floor of my dark bedroom. I laid there still praying to get unnoticed and that my mother would be okay.

After listening closely, I could hear a man ask my mother "Where is she?" But my mother didn't reply. Now my fear of being found had become full force terror. Because I knew then that my mother didn't want me found either.

I wanted to run in hide but I couldn't move. I just laid there praying I was having a dream. But before I knew it my bedroom door flung open and my lights were switched to on. And then I felt a hand feeling around in the bed. "Sahara it's okay. We're not here to hurt you. Come on out!!!" an unknown woman spoke. My cover was blown literally.

"Hey Baby, where are you?" boo asked. He shielded the detrimental vision I try to forget.

I wiped the tear from my eye. I was relieved that I decided against makeup for the day. I watched his feet from beneath the bed. I hoped he would miss my one abandoned pump near the night stand. The sooner he would see me entirely dressed the sooner I could take off my pumps and put them back in storage.

Just like a man he half looked and assumed I wasn't there. Which I was grateful he did. He went back down the steps. I tiptoed over for my shoe, trying not to make his hardwood floors squeak. I ran my fingers across my hair and glanced in the dresser mirror.

Beautiful smooth sepia skin. A 63-inch giant, 36-28-42-dimensional framework. Exotic lips dressed with gloss. Long, jet black, thick hair. Slicked back in a low ponytail to avoid interference. Not a strand out of place.

Looking like a prospect for Ebony magazine's cover. Breast soft and perky in my Vicki S. latest edition. But soft, jiggly and plump. The perfect peach! Leaving a trail of Nina Ricci scent everywhere I roamed. Body lathered in baby oil glistening like a new diamond. Sporting a day's young manicure and pedicure topped off with an OPI's shade of Spring Lavender. All set for my man tool.

I must have been too in my thought and missed hearing his footsteps and the door fling open.

"There goes my baby (oooo girl look at you)" in his singing voice, replicating Usher Raymond's hit song.

I stood roughly six feet away from him. I did a complete 360 pivot in turtle motion showcasing his birthday gift.

"Happy Birthday! You like," I rhetorically questioned?

He licked his lips and held out his arms. "Forget like, I love it!"

I walked to him in a brisk pace. We embraced. I wouldn't let him go.

I needed his comfort more than anything.

I learned a long time ago that the wisest thing I can do is be on my own side be an advocate for myself and others like me

-MAYA ANGELO

THREE

December 1997

Time: 0352

Cleveland, Ohio

SAHARA WATCHED HER MOTHER FROM THE BACKSEAT OF the black unmarked police car. Sahara knew that her mom was in some sort of trouble but she couldn't think of any reason off the top of her head. Sahara couldn't understand why her mom was not speaking to her. *Where are they taking her,* she thought?

Violet walked in handcuffs in between two male cops.

Sahara knocked repeatedly, harder and harder, on the backseat driver window as loud as she could without hurting her small fist but Violet never looked her way. *Why won't she look at me,* she thought.

So, she yelled: "Ma… ma, mommy," but still no reply. Sahara pulled at the door handle. *Its locked!* Sahara tried shoving the door with her shoulder and pulling the handle simultaneously. No luck.

By now, Violet was placed in the black and white cop car. The cops signaled for the social worker to pull off. Sahara tried again to knock on the window but this time with both hands and even harder.

The social worker was talking but Sahara wasn't listening. She made an attempt to offer somewhat of an explanation but by this moment it was too late.

Sahara was spaced out, scared, confused and in raged, watching Violet from the rear window until the car faded from view. Violet never did look back.

Case number: 121797001-OH

Date: 17 December 1997

Reporting Officer: SGT Thomas

Incident Type: Drug Possession, Child Neglect

Location: 1971 East 71st Street, Cleveland, OH 44103

Witnesses: Unknown;

(Anonymous tip made to Child Abuse Hotline)

Evidence: Drug Paraphernalia

Description of Occurrence:

Sergeant Jones and Thomas respond to a dispatch call of possible drug transaction and child neglect on East 79th and Chester Avenue intersection at 0324 on December 17, 1997.

Possible woman suspect fitting description given by dispatch seen leaving alleged crime scene and walking alone headed westbound on Chester Ave. Sergeants then patrolled the area and observed the suspect closely. Suspect seen heading southbound on East 71st street to residence. Suspect detained. Suspect's minor child in home alone. Minor female child age 8-10 asleep upon arrival.

Social services in home to transport child to CPS center.

Suspect, Violet Wilcox apprehended 0418. Drug paraphernalia confiscated from suspect person and entered into evidence. No drugs recovered.

Arrived at precinct 0429.

FOUR

Sahara

I HAVE ALWAYS BEEN DIFFERENT. AND NOT TO BE SAID IN A condescending sense. I ask the questions few care to know. *Why is the sky blue? Why is the sky called sky and not grapes? Why do we celebrate birth and mourn death? Why is white cake referred to as Angel food and chocolate cake Devil food?*

I use to want to fit in and be liked until I learned it was okay to be me. It's okay to be unusual. It's okay to be abnormal. There is no right or wrong to who a person is. It may or may not be socially acceptable.

But when I began to learn social acceptance is just a matter of opinion and opinions are just opinions, I looked at my life and those close to me lives and my perspective changed. The metamorphosis from young lady to woman.

My date of birth is on one of the best if not the best days of the year, New Year's Eve. A day to conclude what has past and introduce what's to come.

I was born in the 80s and raised in the 90s. The age of the Walkman, Super Nintendo, Sega Genesis, pogo stick, Skip it, toss and catch and Hip Hop, with the emerge of two of the most influential artists of all time: Tupac and Biggie. And the era of the crack epidemic.

In the 80s and 90s, you were either abusing drugs, selling drugs or negatively impacted by a loved one engaging in either of the two; and crack babies were promised to overpopulate, exhaust our health care with their disabilities and ruin their communities.

I grew up watching nearly a dozen TV series: the Simpsons, Full House, Tales from the Crypt, Pinky and the Brain, Animaniacs, Martin, Moesha, Prince of Bel Air, Family Matters, Saved by the Bell and Sister Sister.

We played outside for hours playing "Nikka Knocka" (a prank game when kids would knock on neighbors' doors in the ghetto and run; kids would get a kick out of the older kids and adults cursing, swearing and getting upset once realizing they were pranked), "That's my Car", "Red light, Green Light", hop scotch, freeze tag and relay racing.

On hot summer days, we got creative and invented are own water splash park, cracking open the Fire hydrant and using our mother's pots and bowls for collecting water.

And with too much time on our hands we sneaked to play "Hide & Go Get It", "House", "Spin the Bottle" and "Truth or Dare".

A time in my life before I acknowledged the grey areas. When I was green as they came.

The time before the before.

FIVE

Nina

I SET BACK AN OBSERVE THE MAN AT THE BAR. HE WAS dressed casual in navy blue khakis, a white polo shirt and a pair of cognac oxfords. He wore a clean shaved head with a low nice trimmed full beard. Look to be late thirties early forties. His hands were strong masculine and clean; his palms callused. He wasn't wearing a watch or jewelry. He set in the best seat in the house, where he could watch the door, watch the bar and watch the 60in TV mounted to the wall.

I had no idea who he was but everyone else seemed to know him. I listened near at the women snickering and pointing his way. I watched the guys swarm around him to greet him. But he always seemed to keep it sweet but short and continued to monitor the door, the bar and the football game. He drank Bacardi Limon on the rocks with a twist of lime and a splash of orange juice. The bartended would pour him another drink like clockwork when his glass would get half full. I never seen him reach to pay nor see the bartender ring in his order on a tab.

I stayed there longer than anticipated because I was intrigued. What should have only been an outing of two drinks turned into five drinks. The bar was near closing and he hadn't moved but once to go to the restroom. Just when I was close to getting restless, he yells out "last call" and walks behind the bar to raise the lights.

As I finished my last drink, I continued to watch him even more closely than before. He hand-signaled for security to begin to round up patrons to leave and then walked over to the DJ and gave him money. He walked around collecting abandoned shot, rock and wine glasses, plastic cups and napkins left behind on the tables; pushing in chairs and picking up large debris from the floor.

He made his way towards me and I attempted to avoid eye contact. I wasn't dressed up to par to make an everlasting first impression. Despite my attempt, we came face to face when he intruded my territory.

"How you doing young lady? You mind if I take those glasses?" he asked.

"I would have taken them up," I smirked shyly.

"No worries but we appreciate it. Everything okay, did you have a bad day today?" He looked concerned.

"No not at all. Why'd you ask?" I asked puzzled.

"Well for starters most women don't travel to a bar at night alone and you've had 5 drinks"

"Well someone pays close attention I see" I blushed, learning that he had noticed me.

"Yes, that's my job. You must watch your business. No one can take care of yours like you" he stated. I smiled because I had heard that before. He reminded me so much of Daddy.

"It's better now" I grinned. I grabbed my keys from the table. "Have a goodnight" I left feeling accomplished. I had had my answer.

Next time, I were to see him I would be ready to make my move, I thought to myself.

Daddy taught me a lot of things. First it was the desire to want more and the idea of entrepreneurship. I also learned a valuable skill of people watching from him. He would always say "You have two ears, two eyes and one mouth for a reason".

Growing up with a father like my father. I heard a lot and seen a lot. Both of which were a blessing and a curse.

As a toddler, I recall bobbing and weaving around my mother torso trying to see what she tried so hard to conceal. Many nights, I would accompany my mother to work at my father's bar, Cecilio's Club 100, which featured go-go dancers. Cecilio's was home to the Saint Clair and Glenville street hustlers in the 80s and 90s.

I was impressed how the Go-Go dancers paraded around in a basic bikini with their mature voluptuous bodies and customers lost control. Cheering and tipping them all night.

Somewhere between five and eight years old, Daddy got the notion to put me to work in his other business, his store. Which I hated then but cherish now.

Daddy put me in charge of the candy inventory. I would let him know every week what candy we needed when it was time to restock at the local warehouses, Seaway, Sam's Club and Hancock's Tobacco and Candy. Daddy's store was every kid's dream come true.

We had 25 cents bags of true penny candy (that he honestly sold for a penny. I know because I had to count 25 frootie tootsie every weekend and bag them in sandwich bags), Mint Juleps, powder sugar straws, candy cigarettes, Chico sticks, Now and Laters, Cry Baby gum, gummy candy mini burgers, gummy candy hot dogs, candy wax lips, Blow Pops, Dum Dum pops, Original Tootsie rolls, Ring Pops, Mary Janes, sour gummy worms, Sour Punch Twist, War Heads, Nerds Rope, Air Heads bar, Bubble Gum tape, Push Pop and Jolly Ranchers. If you wanted it, we had it and if we didn't Daddy made sure he went and got it!

I was also in charge of stocking the pop and juice coolers after we received our shipment.

Also at times when Daddy got busy he would make me sign for his shipment from LaRose and Dan Dee. I would have to verify that Daddy's order was right; the order form and the merchandise better had matched or I would have not heard the last of it and I would have had to answer for it. I had to account for every bag of chips and every case of beer with each deliver.

Daddy would try to sneak out the door and I would I always catch him. Wherever he went it was a must I had to tag along too. I often made rounds with my dad to his other vendors, Deans Supply and Farmhouse Food Distributors as well.

I was fascinated with everything about my dad. I admired how he started from nothing; One of nine kids from Macon, Georgia. He was doing damn well for a black man in his day. A bar, a store, a restaurant and rental homes, he was the shit if I may so myself.

So quite naturally, I was attracted to bosses. I wanted a man like my father or better. Being a manager wasn't good enough. I need the man who owns the building. It was something about the way my father's name and presence commanded respect that I couldn't claim an average John Doe.

Daddy and I would have breakfast at Landmarks on East 55th Street at least once a week. And we had lunch at B&B restaurant on East 105th street 2-3 times a week. I would order the same thing every time: Fried chicken, greens and yams, and hot water cornbread was served with all the meals. The food was good but I didn't like the cornbread. So, I would spread my yams as if it were margarine across my cornbread to conceal its bland taste.

There weren't many things that I could say that I related with my peers but being a Jiffy cornbread fan was one of them. I loved my cornbread sweet like cake.

The waiter would always have Cecilio's cup of coffee with cream and sugar waiting for him by the time we took our seats. She anticipated all our needs before Daddy and I could request them. I fell in love with her treatment of us and every other local waiter and waitress who waited on Daddy and me.

The city loved him and it showed. He was always greeted with smiles, warm welcomes and impeccable service.

At one, I owned my first pair of diamond earrings. My dad told me at nine that he wanted to be the first man to give me a diamond. For three reasons: one, so I would know that he will always be the first; second, I'll know that I deserve the best; and third I wouldn't except any cubic zirconia's.

The gifts from daddy were nonstop.

My daddy found the most expensive and lavish bedroom set he could find one year. A set that was most likely designed for a teenager he had no objection of purchasing it for my 6th birthday.

SIX

Aniya

"WHAT'S UP GIRLY? YOU ROLLING TONIGHT," YASMINE asked?

My classmate had called to touch bases with our plans. She had asked me earlier in the day to hang out with her for her birthday.

Being the legal age to drink wasn't as fun as the underage partying. It was something about sneaking, lying and scamming our way into clubs and/or liquor stores that was thrilling.

Nights my childhood friends and I would plot and scheme outside Vehls on the Circle, The Millennium and Mirage on the Water about how the four or five of us would get in on one official ID card. Thanks to my older, play sister, Tashia.

Those were the good days. But now that I was of age, partying wasn't as impressive. Nevertheless, I am a woman of my word and I promised Yasmine I would go out with her.

"Sure. With all the stress of these darn classes. I need a break from studying. Where we to" I asked in my phony ecstatic voice.

"We in the wind! Cool?"

"I heard that. Where do you wanna meet up?" I asked.

"My place. 250th and Euclid. And you'll hop in with me and we'll go from there," She stated overjoyed that I was really agreeing to a night out in the town with her.

"Okay. I'll call you when I'm outside! 1030 alright?"

"Perfect," Yasmine said.

We bar hopped all night long. I was so glad she drove because I was heavily under the influence. We made it back to her place in the wee hours of the night.

"Hey girl, you want to come in? You're welcome. It's late, you can go home in the morning," Yasmine asked, as I was getting out of her car to get into mine.

"Okay, cool." I hit the remote for my car to unlock my doors. Those six-inch stilettos had run its course. I threw them on my passenger side, lock my doors and headed behind Yasmine in my flip flops.

"Aye, you were shooting all the dudes down tonight," she implied.

"I can't have a serious conversation with them when I know they aren't worth shit" I laughed. "One nut ball had his pants sagging so low that he can barely walk. The other one thought I missed the shiny accessory on his finger. And I almost forgot about Mr. I have this business and that business but didn't offer to buy you a drink not once."

"You are crazy girl" She burst into laughter. "But you know I was good. I don't need a man to buy me anything."

"Hell, me either but certain things separate the men from the boys. The women from the girls and so for and so on. And I dare he brag about his yearly revenue but too cheap to buy an eight dollars drink. I would have respected him more had he not bought me a drink."

We entered her place. I was exhausted and couldn't wait for her to show me where to crash. The room was dim; the only light was from the motion light outside of her home. I had that feeling like someone was watching me. I had lost sight of Yasmine but assumed she went to switch on a lamp. Then I seen movement, a shadow and a woman's silhouette.

She reappeared and stood a few feet in front of me. She stared at me like most men do when they're undressing me with their eyes. I had seen this look a million times over.

If there was ever a woman that I was attracted to she would have definitely been it. Honey brown skin tone, golden brown eyes, big full lips, high Indian cheek bones, shoulder length wavy luxurious sandy brown streaked black hair, perfect milk white teeth, and a "Buffy the Body" body. She dressed sexy but classy. Never revealing. I guess her hour glass shaped was at fault. Even when she wasn't trying she still got attention. Quiet, sweet, easy going and personable. And a closet freak.

She stood behind me gently brushing her crotch area against my behind. I can feel the mid seam of her pants glide across my cheeks. I was aroused. I pretended not to notice. She kissed and then licked my neck, making it hard to ignore her. Part of me wanted her to stop but the other part of me wanted to witness whether the saying was true or not, "Women know, what women want". I guess my silence spoke as consent and acceptance.

She proceeded to run her hands beneath my shirt and under my bra. She licked her fingers and played with my nipples; she twirled, extended and rolled them until they were nice and pointed. She lifted my shirt over my head and began to lick up my spine. She unzipped my jeans and kissed my freshly shaved pubic area styled with a landing strip.

She tugged twice at my jeans and they fell to my knees. While standing and her squatting, she licked my clit uncontrollably. Her precision was even more enticing than the view. She knew how fast to lick, how slow to lick and where to lick. She even knew when to stop by the trembling in my thighs to avoid a speedy climax. She would rise to kiss my stomach and then go back to work.

What was actually twenty minutes felt like an hour of anticipation. It was the most wonderful gratifying torture I had ever experienced. Once she could no longer prolong my climax. She helped me lie down to the plush grey carpet. She massaged every inch of my body with the most concentration on my buttocks. When she reached my ankles, she would lean up to lick my anus. I was convinced that the theory was fact! I had a couple of men who had come close but hands down she took the cake.

She didn't speak and neither did I. The memory makes me quiver. It took me about an hour to get myself together and gather my things. It was time to leave.

I was in utter disbelief that I had done the unthinkable. I had sex with a woman.

I don't know when or how I made it home. I just remember waking up naked on the floor of the kitchen with a cold half eaten leftover slice of pizza in my hand.

If you don't program your mind, someone will do it for you

–LES BROWN

SEVEN

Winter 2001

Cleveland, Ohio

Winter Break

Sahara

I HAD GONE TO LOOK FOR MY MOTHER ONE EVENING AT ONE of her old hangouts and was taken away by what I saw.

I hadn't seen my mother in over a month and wanted badly just to hug and be held by her. Violet had really gone off the deep end after losing custody of my brother and I. But Violet made sure she called to check in on me daily. And when I hadn't heard from her in two days, I began to think the worse; she overdosed and is somewhere dead in alley, where no one knows she there; or maybe she owed her dealer and he came back for vengeance; or even worse she had decided to completely vanish and abandon me for good.

I caught two buses, the #15 to the #6, to get to Violet's old stepping grounds. I knocked twice with no answer and tried the knob before I decided to head to the back door. Of course, the back door was locked as well. I went for the kitchen window that set adjacent to the back door; and to my surprise it was unlocked. I crawled my way in through the window in hopes of being undetected.

It was obvious that someone was living there but it was in no way healthy or sanitary for any human to be residing there. There were no electricity or heat.

There was old worn unkempt furniture present. The apartment reeked of urine, feces, garbage, spoiled matter and dope.

Apparently, whoever lived there was there illegally because the toilet was backed up with assuming weeks of feces and urine. Coffee tables decorated with crack dust, charred table spoons and broken antennas (used as a makeshift stem), balled up pieces of copper Brillo pads and fast food carryout containers.

The only sign of my mother was a red pair of the old-school ear muffs with the hard-plastic head piece; I had bought her for Christmas one winter.

I wasn't sure how long ago she had been there or if she was coming back or if she was even still alive. But I was prayerful that if I would leave a note or something to show that I came searching for her that someone would give her the message if she would not have returned.

I pulled an orange highlighter from my purse along with an old McDonald's receipt and left my mom a note that read: Love u ma, call me Sahara.

Two more days went by before I heard from my mother. She told me that she had been staying with a friend that I had never met, not too far from the home I had visited two days prior.

Violet also explained that she went back to the home after she realized she had left her ear muffs that I had brought her and found the note.

Violet was without a question strung out on drugs but she still loved us, her children dearly. She tried her best to keep what little she had to remind her of her children. Violet kept a beat-up wallet of pictures of me and my older brother, Jason.

EIGHT

Sahara

JASON AND I WERE FIVE YEARS APART. WE HAD DIFFERENT fathers. Other than my mother and father he was all I had and I was all he had. His father was absent.

It's strange how as children you don't realize at the time the flaws of your parents. It's not until you're a teenager and young adult that you realize, *hey somethings not right with this picture!*

Violet was lacking in her nurturing motherly capabilities which was no mystery to anyone by a long shot. But what outsiders didn't know is that she tried to protect Jason and I from harm as best she could.

I recalled my mother hanging a curtain in the door frame of the living room to conceal her and her buddies getting high. Most days Jason and I would be well asleep.

If it was earlier in the day, Violet would make us go outside and play; or make her John give her money to give to us to leave and go eat dinner at one of several fast food restaurants at Church Square, a shopping plaza about a half mile from our apartment.

She never allowed strays and fiends to be in our home unattended. If her company stayed in the bathroom too long she was coming to be sure they hadn't wander into one of our rooms.

If my mother hadn't taught me anything, she did teach me survival. Days there weren't much food, Jason and I made do with "government" cheese and saltine crackers, ramen noodles, sugar, syrup, or P&J sandwiches. On better days, it was chips, cookies, juice and/or tuna fish sandwiches. On really scarce days, Jason and I ate Swiss milk chocolate coco packets and Kool Aid packets mixed with sugar in its dry form.

And she always had potatoes. A ten-pound bag of potatoes went along way; we made baked potatoes, fries, hash browns, scalloped potatoes, sautéed potatoes or mashed potatoes.

Violet would volunteer at the local Salvation Army's soups kitchen (a place where free hot lunch is served daily to the hungry/ unfortunate) to get the day's leftovers and anything else staff was willing to give her.

My mother would also frequent the church food pantries for donated non-perishable goods such as hamburger helper, Spaghettios, Ravioli, oatmeal, grits, box cold cereal and canned fruits, vegetables and meat: tuna, sardines, Spam and Vienna sausages.

In the winter, when our electricity would be disconnected for a week or so, my mother kept a house full of flashlights and candles. We would use the porch as a refrigerator for are food. We had a small battery operated table top TV and radio.

My mother would donate blood for cash some months.

But most weeks I lived a double life between my parents. My father had made my mother promise "not to put them white folks in their business" way before I was born. And a promise she kept.

In doing so, Violet never received child support for me but in return I stayed with my father on weekends, holidays, summer, spring and winter breaks/vacations.

The time spent with my father, I was treated like a princess. Among other things, my father was widely known for being a phenomenal chef. Five course, homecooked meals and feast were on the menu everyday with my father, more than likely where my exquisite taste in food came to surface. The best in Cleveland if you asked me.

You name it, he cooked it! From down home southern dishes to a seafood lover's paradise, I had it my way. He served smothered chicken, fried chicken, fried Walleye, grilled salmon, oven roast and gravy, King crab legs, frog legs, scampi and lobster to T-bone steaks and filet mignon, green beans and potatoes, mac and cheese, candied yams, black-eyed peas, collard, mustard and turnip greens, twice baked potato, peach cobbler, pound cake and sweet potato pie.

I also had great memories of my mom too.

I remember my mother taking Jason and I around the city to see the Christmas lights. We would ride the bus from downtown Public Square to the GE building in East Cleveland. And every year, General Electric Company out did themselves from the previous season.

She would always find some free or discounted activity for us to do. We would go swimming and or roller skating at the local Salvation Army. And on Mondays we went to the show for half off admission and free popcorn.

At the first of the month when are food assistance reloaded, Violet would always buy a couple boxes of brownies for Sunday desert. Man, she made the best brownies; crunchy exterior with a warm gooey interior. And whoever was the first to the sink, the mixing bowl was fair game.

During snowfall in the winter we would build snowmen, make snow angels and have snowball fights.

When I was sick, she would nurse me back to health with all the old-school remedies; Campbells Chicken noodle soup, Verners Ginger Ale, saltine crackers, OJ, Vicks vapor rub and some good ole TLC. She would rub my belly or my back until I fell asleep and snuggled me in a blanket next to her.

Violet, Jason and I would occasionally have family night every few weeks. We would play board games and watch Blockbuster movie rentals, before the days of Internet, Netflix and Hulu. We had a pretty decent selection of games: Sorry, Connect 4, Operation, Life, Jenga, Trouble and UNO.

A small part of me, the present woman I am still loved and embraced the good memories; while the other me dared to be unforgiving in remembrance of the days that turned into months, and the months into years, that I waited for that call from her to tell me, "Pack up, I'm coming to get you".

I've learned that people will forget what you said, people will forget what you did, but people will never forget how you made them feel."

-MAYA ANGELOU

NINE

December 1997

Child Protective Services

THE OLDER GENTLEMEN PACED THE WHITE TILE FLOOR with his hands in his coat pockets. He appeared to be anxious and concerned.

"Mr. Ramal, she is resting in our holding area," the counselor reassured the man. "She seems to be holding up well considering all that has happened. She is under constant surveillance. She's a tough cookie. Any other kid would be balling their eyes out about now. But she is doing surprisingly good."

"What do I need to do? Can I see her?"

"Well, first thing first we need to establish her a temporary residence and guardian. Are you seeking to take over custody of your daughter?"

"I will if I have to. But she needs a mother figure. I'm single and a business man. I work 18-20 hours of the day, 7 days a week."

"Does the child have any other next to kin that you see fit to raise her?"

"Her mother's dad and his wife. Violet, Sahara's mother called me this morning. She wants her with her grandparents in Warrensville Heights," Mr. Ramal stated.

"Terrific. I know you expressed your wishes to see Sahara. But I don't think it is in the best interest of the child to see you if she is not being turned over to your custody. I have seen things go terribly bad when it's time for the visit to end and to separate. Although, I can allow you to observe her through a two-way mirror and/or real time camera if you desire."

"Understood! I'll get on calling her grandparents after I see her," Mr. Ramal consented to the counselor's recommendations.

TEN

Sahara

I LOOKED DOWN AT MY LEFT LEG AND IT WAS GONE. I HAD started writing on my limbs to keep track of the days, dates and times. I assumed I was going crazy initially until I would wake up and my writing would be removed.

I began dating myself like a person would date a Ziploc bag of food being stored in the freezer. I would note the first two initials of the day, the date and military time, like so: Sa 3/10 2100 as to notate Saturday March 10th at 9pm.

I did this to determine whether I was dreaming or not. I would choose a different location on one of my four extremities daily.

I could no longer tell my dreams from reality. It all felt real.

And when my writings would disappear, I came to accept that my dreams were in fact reality. I was the only person who knew where I marked myself, therefore I had to be the one removing it.

But how could this be true. What I was experiencing was something out of a therapist's manual.

Am I crazy? Am I insane? Am I nut job? Am I psychotic?

Who am I? I wasn't just Sahara, I was someone else.

ELEVEN

February 2000

Tower City Cinema

Cleveland. Ohio

Aniya

MY BUDDIES AND I WERE UP TO NO GOOD. WE HAD THE entire day mapped out. We were going to catch a movie, get high, clown and make it back home all in time before the street lights came on.

To ensure the night was everything we had hope we packed a bag of goodies. The goodies includes were a 4 pack 8 ounce can of Steele Reserve 211, 22 ounce St. Ides kiwi strawberry, pint of Wild Irish Rose, pack of Cherry Blends and Black 'n Milds, two philly cigar blunts, a dime bag of dro, two $1 bags of Flamin' Hots Cheetos, two 25¢ Ranch Doritos, two 25¢ Funyuns, two 25¢ Nacho Cheese Doritos, two 25¢ Dan Dee Salt and Vinegar chips, two Pina Colada Faygo 16 ounce pops, two 16 ounce Tahitian Treats, two Reese cups, one Snickers, one Butterfinger, one original Skittles and a bag of penny candy.

We caught the #1 bus to Tower City. We made it all the way to the front doors of the theater and chickened out when we seen CPD in front of the entrance.

Instead of the risk of getting caught, we went back to my girl, Marcita's house. Marcita's home was the hang out; she had a single mom whom was always gone at work.

We popped in "Set It Off" for the hundredth time but it never got old. My girls and I kicked back, watch the movie and got busted. I didn't smoke but I enjoyed the drank.

There wasn't a dry eye in the room after Cleo went out blazing like Scarface. It was something about the underdog never standing a chance that bothered young me.

All they wanted was a better life. They didn't ask to be poor. What's going to happen to Tee Tee's baby? Damn! Another kid raised by the system. Why everybody had to die and leave Stony alone? What good is all the money in the world with no one to share it with?

I drifted off to sleep until it was time to head home.

TWELVE

Three hours,

Forty minutes later

Sahara

MY HEAD WAS SPINNING AND MY SPIT TASTED AWFUL. I could smell my breath. It stunk. This had become a pattern over the last year.

The same smell, the same taste as before. And the nagging headache.

I looked around and Marcita was passed out on the floor and her friend lying sleep on the opposite end of me on the couch.

I couldn't remember how I got to Marcita's. Last thing I remembered was watching "Set It Off" at home.

I went to her restroom and gargled with warm water and washed my face. I shuffled through the empty beer cans, candy wrappers and chip bags for my keys and coat.

I had an hour to make it home by curfew. I told Marcita, I would see her later and she mumbled something under breath and turned over on her stomach.

I walked a quarter mile to the nearest bus stop. The next bus was due to arrive in a couple minutes.

THIRTEEN

June 2000

Summer Break

Cleveland, Ohio

Aniya

"HEY GIRL," MARCITA ANSWERED THE PHONE.

"What you doing," I asked with curiosity.

"My boyfriend just came over," she quickly replied. In other words: I don't have time to talk.

"Okay girl. Well call me later"

"Alright girl," she rushed to hang up the phone.

Marcita was two years older than me. She was what the elders called "hot in the ass". Heck we all were. But she really really was. She had had more penis then a jock strap. She had a different boyfriend every month. And to make matter worst, she was already a mother.

Her son was in the custody of his paternal grandmother. If I hadn't known Marcita I wouldn't had known she was a mother.

I enjoyed hanging out with her though. She knew how to have fun. But getting drunk and passing out every weekend was getting redundant.

And Sahara wasn't going to tolerate it much longer.

I wanted more action. More thrill. I wanted to experience euphoria at its maximum. And give Sahara ass a legitimate reason to be upset.

June 21, 2000

The day I became a woman. I didn't know what that meant, just that Marcita and the older teenagers would say this. I waited for this burst of excitement and addictive high that I had heard women speak about. But that feeling never came.

His named was Ed, shortened for Edward. But I had nicknamed him "Mr. Eyes" for his forest green eyes. Same age as me.

Smooth even butterscotch skin tone, cocoa brown curly hair, average height and built and a smile that would persuade any girl into saying "yes".

Despite his looks, he left me disappointed and cheated. I was robbed of the unforgettable sensational milestone of becoming a woman.

He needed a structural review of the woman's anatomy. He did six pushups above me and it was over. I didn't feel anything; and I didn't see anything. No pop, no blood, no nothing!

Something can't be right, I thought. *That can't be what they gossip about!*

Sahara

I found a white, transparent, jelly like matter in my underwear. It had a strange odor. It couldn't have been mine because it was on everything, the outside of my shirt and my pants.

Semen!! It had to be. I had learned about it in Health class.

It can't be true! I won't believe it... I am still pure! What is going on? Something's wrong with me. I am crazy!

Everything that glitter ain't gold

-AUTHOR UNKNOWN

FOURTEEN

ne·glect

To disregard or ignore; to fail to perform a duty or to give due attention or care.

Sahara

I WENT FROM SLEEPING ON A QUEEN SIZE MATTRESS SET IN my own room to sharing a room with my aunt on the top bunk of her twin bunk bed.

It's said to be too much burden and responsibility to take on an additional person in one's household. But my grandparents stood up to the challenge. They accepted custody of me when no one else would.

However, I was reminded every day that I didn't belong there which fueled my resentment for Violet.

What mother could turn her back on her young and be content with someone else raising them? Did she think she was that unfit and that anyone else would be better for the job than her? Did she consider how I would feel?

Did the anonymous tipper, who turned my mother in, have good intent? Did he/she truly care about my well-being or was it a vendetta?

"I raised my damn kids, I shouldn't have to raise anyone else's." A statement my grandmother swore by. And she was in all fairness correct.

Why should she have had to raise someone else's child? Every man and every woman should take accountability for their decisions and actions.

In contrary, no child should be made to feel unwanted, a burden and different.

FIFTEEN

Sept 11, 2001

Junior High School

Eighth grade

Sahara

I WAS IN CLASS HALF A SLEEP AS USUAL. NOTHING SAID IN A classroom interest me anymore. My dad was a college dropout and he had more money than anyone I had ever known. I would go through the hoops just because I knew I had too and it looked good.

The younger me wanted to finish school to one up my mom and prove all the naysayers wrong; but I was unenthusiastic about any lesson on the syllabus. I did the minimum to pass the course to go on to the next grade to graduate.

And out of nowhere comes my Home Ed teacher busting through the door screaming

"Say it's not so!" She screamed in fright. Scrambling around the teacher desk searching for the remote to the TV mounted to the wall of our classroom.

Everyone just stared at the black screen waiting to see what her fuss was about. And without her flipping to any particular channel the headlines flashed in bold letters "**Aircraft Strikes Trade Center**".

As we watched the live broadcast the second plane hit. Nervous and fearful for her own safety the news anchor couldn't contain her composure. She wanted to run for her life and drop that damn microphone. All her articulate rehearsed dialect had fell by the waist side. She was scared to death and it showed. But she was committed to completing her sector.

Meanwhile at my school, parents were flocking in by the boat load picking up their children or just wanting to lay eyes on them to ensure that they were safe. No one came for me and a few others.

But subsequently school was dismissed. I walked 3 miles, angry. *Don't nobody give a fuck about me.* I reached my grandparents home and just as I expected; everyone was minding their own business making no acknowledgement of my presence.

I greeted my grandparents and carried on to my bedroom.

SIXTEEN

I WAS THE POSTER CHILD FOR A DADDY'S GIRL. DADDY WAS my first love. He showed me the good life before I even knew what it meant.

And for that reason, I was often the target of envy. Friends and family would warn, "he will not always be here to spoil her" or "I will hate to see what she'll do when he's gone".

A warning I ignored.

Daddy's health began to deteriorate suddenly. Doctors said it was prostate cancer that had metastasized to his bone but I say it was heartbreak.

Daddy had finally met his match. A person more powerful and wealthier than him, the city's mayor.

When he refused to sell his businesses and homes, then came the inspectors and violations and then eminent domain. And just like that all his sweat, blood and tears were in vain. I could only imagine what my father felt to have his most prize possessions taken from him one after another until he had nothing left.

As I drive down our old neighborhood, I am consumed with fury and disgust when I look at the other neighboring businesses still standing. Why did they have to take his, ours, mine? Those businesses are in no better shape than what my dad's was in. The only difference is the face who owns them.

Daddy fought hard but ultimately his money ran out. Through it all I never seen him breakdown, give up or cry.

And to think of it, I had never seen my daddy cry even when I knew for sure that he would: after hearing the news that his only son, his protégé had been killed. Genori, Cecilio's second born child had lived a life so many young men, especially black, fall victim too: a drug lord. The lack of resources, lack of patience, lack of education and need for money are the key ingredients for an unfavorable and disreputable livelihood.

Genori climbed the ladder of the drug game swiftly against the advice of his dad. Genori became loved by women and hated by men. Gold diggers and groupies were dying to get a chance with him while jack boys (robbers) and small time block boys plotted on taking his spot.

Cecilio had once told his son that he wasn't cut for the drug game. He told him that, "If he wasn't ready to kill than he better be ready to die". Words that he would later come to regret.

It pays the cost to be the boss

-B.B. KING

SEVENTEEN

Summer 2002

Maple Heights, Ohio

Summer Break

Aniya

I MET MY BEST FRIEND. TIFFANY, MY PARTNER IN CRIME; WE were Thelma and Louise. The summer was ours, we ran the city looking for excitement and chasing men, preferably dope boys.

Dope boys knew how to party and blowing money was a habit they had that we loved.

We would hang out at gas stations, especially "Club Marathon" (the nickname we gave it) on East 55th street; Scouting for brothas with rides.

We attended almost every local car show and festival. Our favorite was Woodhill's car show.

And weekends we would sneak out the house to hang out at the food trailer on East 105th street after hours.

Tiffany was a savage with sticky fingers. She would go to Burlington, TJ Maxx or Marshalls and spend $50 and come out with $200 worth of merchandise. She was the queen of switching tags.

She was good for jacking her dope boy boyfriends too. She would spend the night and sneak in their stash and peel off a couple hundred dollars without them noticing or take an ounce of their weed if she could; she would take half for her personal use and sell the rest.

Tiffany could be a motha___ but I knew if I didn't have anyone else I could always call Tiffany. She was down for whatever whenever. Once, during an afterschool fight she chopped off all a girl's mid back length hair with a pair of scissors. When Tiffany was done with her, her hair was too short to pull into a ponytail.

Tiffany was ruthless. She loved who she loved and said screw everyone else. But I still loved her like a sister. She was who she was and I accepted her.

This cold sense of being was shared by us both; most likely due to our mothers' absence. But Tiffany's character was amplified x 10. We lacked that nurturing, caring, compassionate quality that most girls possessed.

Tiffany was being raised by her father and her mom was M.I.A. We both suffered from "mommy issues".

We were very much different in our own way and didn't agree on a lot of things but one belief we had in common was 'if we wanted it we had to go out and get it ourselves because no one else would".

Tiffany could size up a man in a matter of seconds. She knew how much money he had, whether he was blue or white collar man and/or was he giving or stingy. She watched for the knots in his pockets, his watch and shoe game.

She even knew the cost of paint jobs on cars. If a guy was being boastful, flashing his car, opening doors and "stunting" by her, he better had come correct because she knew the real from the fake.

We were inseparable. We shared many first times together.

Our first spurt of trouble, we were nearly arrested but it was epic. One weekday afternoon, teenage boredom struck. We found ourselves walking down Warrenville Center Road looking for fun. We landed at Giant Eagle at Southgate Shopping Center.

I bet Tiffany that she couldn't catch me on the motorized handicap shopping cart.

I hopped in one parked cart at the entrance way and Tiffany followed behind me in the next available handicap shopping cart. We chased each other down every aisle in the store until that became boring.

We went out to the parking lot, where we started being chased by the old aged toy cop. Too old to keep up, we left him huffing and puffing in the parking lot.

Tiffany and I made it about a half a mile up the street before the batteries died in the carts. By this time, Maple Heights police were on our tail.

I tried to take off running. I stopped when the cop yelled out to me. I wasn't sure whether his weapon was drawn but I knew a joy ride and some excitement wasn't worth my life. I heard of some kids being killed for much less.

Tiffany and I put our hands up and faced the cop.

"What the hell are y'all doing?" the policeman asked. We made eye contact with each other and burst out in laughter. He scolded us.

No charges were filed but the cop wanted to escort us home to notify our guardians and ensure we wouldn't partake in any additional mischief.

A month's punishment… it was all worth it!!! We both whispered to one another in the back seat of the police car on our way home.

I could write a memoir on our numerous of voyages thru adolescence alone.

EIGHTEEN

Spring 2003

High school

Freshman year

Nina

SHE SMIRKED AND SNICKERED AT THE WRONG BITCH today! See these suburb bitches don't know, I'll fight they asses in a New York minute, and have they ass running to their mommas with they boogie, sadity, "don't want for nothing" asses!...... Sahara too busy wanting everyone to like her, but not me!

I chanted to myself as I went to smack the taste out of my classmate's face. I had finally caught her alone in the bathroom. *I bet she not so tough now.*

And it was on. We wrestled and tussled across the girls' bathroom for about 10 minutes which felt like thirty minutes. The bell rings.

I rushed to the door to leave before there could be any witnesses but it was too late. My victim was right behind me running to the principal's office.

"Look what she did to my face!" she yelled. "Sahara Ramal".

Stupid bitch! Who would want to tell and get suspended! Fucking Dummy! I can't afford to get suspended again!! Damn!!

Mr. Walker, one of four assistant principals was standing in front of the office glass door. He motioned with his index finger for me to come to him.

Sahara is going to be pissed once she learns we're suspended again. I walked peacefully to the office, promising to catch my enemy again outside of school! I was all too familiar with the principal's office. I had been suspended too much to keep count.

We were very bright but I had a bad temper. I was eager to release my tension on anyone who gave me a reason and especially anyone who messed with my Sahara.

"Miss Ramal," Mr. Walker stated. He shook his head with disappointment. "What's the reason this time?"

"How many days I got? Three or five?" I asked ignoring his question. Secretly, I had grown tired of my own behavior also.

"I don't think that's the answer miss lady. Suspension isn't teaching you anything! I want you to go see Mrs. Brooks-Thornton"

Mrs. Brooks-Thornton was the only female assistant principal but was known for being just as hard on the girl students as she were the boy students, if not harder.

On the walk, down to her office, I thought about my punishment. *They can't expel me. I'm not that bad. I didn't really hurt her for real.* I knocked on her door.

"Come in," Mrs. Brooks-Thornton instructed. I entered, closing the door behind me. I set down in the seats facing the principal's desk. "Well hello Sahara, what do I owe this visit?"

"Mr. Walker told me to come see you"

"Why does he want me to see you," she questioned?

"I was fighting in the bathroom a few minutes ago,"

"And why were you fighting Sahara"

"She been saying what she a do to me, so I called her bluff," I smirked.

"I don't think that anything is funny Sahara. This is your life you're playing with. What would you have done had you hit that girl in her head the wrong way and she died? What would you had told her family? What would you had told your family? What would have been your defense in the court of law? Do you think they would have accepted you saying: you were calling her bluff? What's wrong with you? Do you need to talk to someone? Is something bothering you?

"I don't know," I responded with tears in my eyes. No one had ever spoke to me in that tone and with genuine concern.

"What do you want to do with your life? Don't you want to make your parents proud of you? You are a young woman. You will be grown soon you cannot continue to behave like this!"

"I don't know."

Life after high school wasn't my concern at this point. I was in my freshman year and I hadn't thought about it for a single minute. Sahara had played around on the school newspaper in middle school but it didn't go pass that. Nothing else interest us.

We were still in denial about Cecilio's health. His condition had a poor prognosis with an expectancy of 4 months to live.

"Miss Ramal, I am going to do you a favor because underneath that hard shell I think you're a good girl with great potential. I am going to suspend you for 5 days in hopes that you get your act right. If not, next time you come before me it will be an expulsion." She looked in my eyes with utter sincerity.

"Upon returning to school, you will start a daily journal expressing your emotions. You need to release all this hostility you have. You will enroll in either a trade or tech program of your choice. And you will submit an essay for next month's National City Bank's African American essay competition; entitled What Does Black History Mean to Me. Understood?"

"Yes!"

NINETEEN

Saturday,

June 14, 2003

Summer Break

THE DAY BEFORE FATHER'S DAY, I STOOD IN FRONT OF THE bathroom mirror brushing my hair and looking over myself. I wore a white sleeveless blouse with black polka dots, a black skirt and black strap scandals.

The limo ETA was in 15 minutes. I started to think of ways I could avoid having to leave. *What if I stayed in here and didn't go" "Would anyone notice I was missing?"* I thought. Seconds later I could hear Caren calling my name.

Caren, Cecilio's oldest child from a previous relationship, was more of a "cool aunt" than a sister. She was old enough to be my mother but we were still close like siblings.

Caren's children were nearly my age. Despite the age difference, Caren and I shared a lot in common. We both had strong personalities, independent and genuine daddy's girls. We knew our worth but we were the furthest away from being the women we knew we could be.

"Sahara, you ready! let's go!"

I didn't reply.

"Sahara…Sahara, where is she?" Caren asked other relatives in the house.

Realizing there was no other choice but to come forward. I opened the door to the bathroom.

"Yeah"

"You alright, it's time!" Caren stated.

I nodded and proceeded to follow behind Caren.

The entire car ride I wondered what I was heading in to. *How would he look? How would he smell? Who would be there to wish him farewell? Would I be a chameleon like I have always been?* Adapting to every situation at any given time. *Would people finally see me fold and crack under pressure?*

The entire service was a blur. I set inches from the casket not wanting to accept my reality. *I was dreaming,* I thought. *It's a dream it must be. He looked like my dad and all his family and friends were present. It has to be real. Pinch me somebody!*

"Ashes to ashes, dust to dust," the minister quoted.

The funeral staff gathered around the corpse. They folded the casket linen over his face and chest; then closed the casket.

"Will the pallbearers proceed to the front, please" asked the minister.

And in that second all strength escaped me. I couldn't hold back another tear! I could no longer close my mouth tight to conceal my sob.

He was really dead. My daddy, my first love, my hero was dead.

I cried uncontrollably until my eyes were sore and all cried out. I couldn't breathe. I started to hyperventilate to regain air but I couldn't catch my breath.

I ran to the door for fresh air. And I looked to my right and my mother was standing there beside me rubbing my back.

TWENTY

Fall 2003
High school
Sophomore year

Aniya

I SKIPPED MY AFTERNOON CLASSES AND WENT BY MY BOYfriend's house. I had acted it out over and over again in my head how I would break the news to him that I wanted to end things. But nothing I predicted came close to what took place.

We met a week or so after the death of my father. I imagined he would take it rough because like me he really had no one else. We both had dysfunctional families.

Things had gotten too deep but I hated to let go of that bomb sex.

I had planned to be as normal as possible. I set back on the bed and watched television. A few hours went by and I eventually broke the ice.

"I need to talk to you," I cleared my throat.

"What's up?" He asked never turning his head from the television.

"You know I love you, right?" I stuttered. My palms were sweaty.

"Sahara, I don't have no money right now. I told you I got you in a few days". He assumed he knew where I was going with the conversation.

"No I don't need any money!" I said. Mone confirmed he had no clue about what was about to hit him.

"I have to get my life together. I'm messed up. I need to figure some things out"

"I'm sorry about your dad. Things will get better" he promised.

"I don't want to be with you anymore Mone," I grew tired of beating around the bush.

"What," he questioned and turned to face me and looked into my eyes.

"I need to get my life together," I grabbed for my things. And a calm Mone sprouted up and dashed pass me out of the room. I couldn't fathom what it was he was rushing to do. He returned and sat arm length away from me.

"You think I'm just going to let you go like that" he laughed. He laid an impregnated sock across his lap. Mone turned the sock upside down to reveal its contents. And there dropped two bullets and a small revolver.

My eyes grew large. I let out a huge sigh. I have had a brush with death a couple times before but not to this extent.

Trying to keep calm and think fast; I thought of ways to sway his next move. He stood 5'10 at 160lbs, I knew I couldn't out fight him. He had a reputation for backing the best of the best in a corner. I figured I could possibly out smart him.

"If you love me like you say you do, you should want the best for me. Don't you want me to be successful? Graduate and go to college." I placed my hand on his shoulder.

"You think I'm stupid Sahara. If I can't have you, can't nobody have you!" He loaded one bullet and spin the cylinder several times. He stood in front of me and placed the barrel to my skull.

"My family and friends will miss me and they'll come looking for me," I pleaded.

"Let's see if God is on your side." He said with teary eyes. I silently prayed; looking into Mone's eyes, hoping he'll see my despair and renege on his threat.

He pulled the trigger. *Click!* Russia Roulette style. I clutched my eyes shut. To say the least, God was on my side! I pushed passed Mone and sprinted for the door.

I abandoned all my belongings. I ran in the rain coat less and barefoot a mile and a half to the nearest bus stop. I dreaded getting on the bus without shoes and feared disease and illness but anything was better than being dead at that point.

The entire ride people stared and snickered at the crazy girl on the bus with the wet and wild curly hair (what a way to ruin a wrap), drenched clothes and no shoes.

Thankfully I had stopped at the store earlier that day and placed spare change in my pocket or else all my money would've still been in my purse at Mone's; and I wouldn't have had bus fare. I pondered what story I could fabricate to tell my grandparents if they asked.

Needless to say, when I made it home, no one asked and I didn't tell; Which started to become a trend.

If there is no enemy within the enemy outside can do us no harm

-AFRICAN PROVERB

TWENTY-ONE

July 1997

Cleveland, Ohio

Summer Break

Sahara

IT HAD BEEN THREE MONTHS SINCE JASON HAD LEFT. JASON had run away from home. He had bounced from girl's house to friend's house; whoever would allow him to crash on the sofa or floor for the night.

Nights he found nowhere to go, he slept on RTA buses until the driver would kick him off and then he would sleep at the rapid terminal or Greyhound bus station on 13th and Chester, playground of the drug smugglers, prostitutes, runaways and delinquents.

Our trio was divided. He had abandoned me.

I went into Jason's bedroom and laid across his bed faced down smelling his pillow. My mother hadn't changed his room a bit. It was exactly how he left it the night he never came home. I laid there in agony wondering why life had become so dreadfully boring and lonely.

I missed getting off the school bus and seeing Jason there waiting for me. I missed him kicking me out of his room. I had no one to tuck me in when my mother was away for the evening.

I stood up and looked out the window of our five-story high rise apartment building, at the neighbors playing dodge ball with their siblings outside my apartment window.

I opened the window and sat on the window pane and window ledge. I flung my right leg out and then my left while holding on to the window frame.

I set in silence imagining, *what would happen if I jumped? Would Jason come back if he were to learn I was hurt? If I were to die and leave him, would he miss me like I was missing him?*

Before any of my questions could be answered, my mother came in and intercepted it. She pulled me from the window in a panic.

TWO YEARS EARLIER…

Before the days of aggressive child passenger safety laws, Camille and I were sitting together in the front passenger seat of my daddy's 1990 Ford LTD station wagon. Camille, daddy's baby girl, his fourth child of four children.

I was sitting next to the door when the door flung open, to no fault of my own, while daddy driving 50 mph on the freeway in Deadman's Curve. I dangled from the car. The only thing saving me from falling out completely is my tennis shoes being tangled in the lap belt.

The skin from my right palm shredded off during impact. Daddy reached over without a second thought grabbing my feet and pulling me back to safety; all while still controlling the steering wheel of the car.

TWENTY-TWO

Winter 2002

High School

Freshman Year

Nina

I OBSERVED FROM THE SIDE LINES THE RESPECT LEBRON James, then a senior in high school who would later be our opponent in the high school basketball championship, received entering our gymnasium and I was taken away. The Warrensville Heights Tigers were up against one of four of our biggest rival schools, Shaw High Cardinals.

We were also known archrivals of JFK, Shaker Heights and Cleveland Heights High schools.

Shaw had arguably one of the best marching bands next to Glenville TarBlooders, who was also known for their incredible football team. If a player made it into the NFL from Cleveland one could almost bet they came from Glenville, a Cleveland public school.

James didn't need an introduction or a chaperone. Spectators made a path for him to walk and an entire bleacher row for him to sit. They also whispered and stared with admiration.

I couldn't believe the hype over one young man who was just a couple years older than me. I knew at that moment, one day I'll live that life.

I was impressed with the respect and greatness more so than the fame. He was young and possessed a raw talent that most boys fantasied about. A kid could practice day and night and may never come close to being as good as he was.

I had an epiphany that I was gifted, powerful and great beyond measure. I too was unique and special. And one day the world would know it too.

If you want to be somebody, if you want to go somewhere, you better wake up and pay attention

-WHOOPI GOLDBERG

SISTER ACT II

TWENTY-THREE

Nina

LIVING WITH SAHARA HAD BECOME A NUISANCE. ANIYA wasn't an issue. She stayed out of my way and I stayed out of hers.

But if I say go left to Sahara, she'd say right. When I think we're on the same page she goes off into her own little world forgetting about me.

She keeps marking on our body. And it's making me mad. I'm tired of coming to her rescue. Every time she's in trouble I stand up for her.

I don't know what this "date and time" mess is about. But I keep washing it off us and she keeps writing it all over again daily.

I don't know what she's trying to prove. Sahara can do whatever in the hell she wants to do with herself on her time but on my time, I want have that foolishness.

I don't understand the big problem. Were different but that's okay. Other people have a few best friends, meanwhile we have each other: Sahara, Aniya and me. Us three is all the friends we need.

TWENTY-FOUR

Aniya

I HAD ONE MOTIVE AND ONE MOTIVE ONLY. SEX! I HAD AN itch that needed scratching. A kitty that needed licking and a void that needed feeling. Mone had been the cream of the croup but he was a loser. I couldn't indulge myself with him any longer. No matter how great the sex was.

He wasn't right for Sahara or me. And Nina could careless either way; if it wasn't about money she didn't care.

I wanted to make love without the love. They can keep all the mushy stuff. I want a good orgasm so I can go about my way.

Equivalent to a drug fiend in search of that first time high that they won't get back; I was no different.

I continued to abuse my drug in hopes of reaching the same bliss as I had with Mone. But time and time again my expectations were buried and the supplier fell short that is until I met Yasmine.

As terrific as Yasmine was she still is not a man. She was fun, exciting and gave me the best oral sex I ever had. The experiment had been completed and checked off as done. That is all it was.

I needed masculinity. I needed to feel a stiff, rock hard penis. The solid torso of a man. I want his mustache to tickle my upper and lower lips and cheeks. I want that strong grip around my throat when I'm being naughty and the base in his voice when he tells me to "shut up and take it."

It took years to feel hypnotized under a tonic clonic seizure, paralyzed, complete cessation and joy, as I did when I was high off sex.

I needed a fix! And Sahara was blocking with her make-believe hopes of finding true love with these average guys.

TWENTY-FIVE

January 2005

High School

Junior Year

Sahara

MRS. BROOKS-THORNTON WAS A BLESSING IN DISGUISE. Thanks to her I start heading in the right direction.

I came in second place in the statewide essay competition. Winning the competition, validated my passion and talent in writing.

I was able to begin nursing assistant training which prepared me to sit for the state exam. Becoming a STNA, increased my wage drastically compared to my Burger King and/or Marc's Supermarket income; And it provided me with job security.

I was introduced to Kia. At first glance Kia and I appeared to be a mismatch. She was sweet, quiet and to herself, easy going not a very big socializer while I on the other hand was outspoken, opinionated and a social butterfly.

I tend to gravitate towards friends with similar backgrounds as mind. But Kia was the closest to normal friend I had. Although she was being raised by her grandmother. Her grandmother alone gave to her more love and support than any child could ask for.

Her mother was still very much present in her life but Kia decided living with her grandmother in the suburbs would be more beneficial than in the city with her mom.

I learned a lot observing Kia. Her grandmother showed her how to cook, clean and all the other female stuff women showed girls. And what I didn't learn from Kia, I learned from the men I dated. They made sure I knew what women were expected to do and what they weren't. And what I didn't learn from the two, I learned through trial and error.

Kia and I were the perfect combo. What I lacked she knew and what she lacked I knew. Kia was a little rough around the edges when it came to men and street smarts but I was there for her like she had unknowingly been there for me. Kia was the most giving person I had ever met. She would give you the shirt off her back if need be.

Every other month, we would go half on the Reebok tennis shoe special at Lady Foot Locker; buy two pair of Reebok classics for $59.99.

We had become really close.

TWENTY-SIX

July 1, 2005

Summer break

Evergreen Memorial

Nina

DADDY'S BIRTHDAY. I DROVE TO VISIT DADDY AT THE CEMetery. I needed to talk to him. I wanted a hug. I needed to hear his voice.

Sahara had been working as a STNA for several months and had managed to get us an apartment, pay for driving school and bought us a starter car, 1996 Pontiac Sunfire.

Sahara sweetheart, Chaz helped her study for our temps and license. Everyday afterschool he picked us up and let her practice driving.

It took me 30 minutes to find Daddy's plot and I still wasn't sure if I was in the exact area. Caren hadn't made it around to getting daddy a headstone yet but I told her not to worry about it because I would buy it.

I sprawled out with my blanket across the grass. I talked to him for hours. My emotions ran rapid. I laughed reminiscing about the good times and cried realizing how he was taken from me too soon.

Daddy helped a lot of people and he gave me the world. I hated to see him go without. He needed a headstone. I owed him that much.

It became my life's mission to see to it that another birthday of his wouldn't pass again without him having one.

Sahara's STNA income had sufficed for awhile but I needed more. I called Chaz to brainstorm.

"Hey cutie, what's going on?" Chaz answered.

"Hey Sexy, Nothing much. Missing you!" I tried to talk like Sahara.

"Oh, for real, say the word and I'm there," he laughed.

"Nah but for real though. I want to ask you something"

"Shoot!"

"Can you get me something like what you got? What's it going to cost me?" I asked. Chaz's uncle was the marijuana connect. Chaz was moving pounds by the day. Sahara had no clue. But I knew better.

There was no way all his money came from cutting hair. He drove the cleanest old school Monte Carlo in high school, wore all the freshest gear and he stayed surprising Sahara with gifts. I overheard him talking on the phone about "grams" one day. And he always kept little bags of weed stashed in his car.

"Bud?" he sounded confused.

"Yeah. One big bag."

'Since when has that became your concern. That's not your thing."

"That's wasn't the question Chaz. I need you to come thru for me"

"Well I'm sorry to let you down, but my people went down. I'm out that life!"

I slammed down the phone in his ear.

I wasn't sure if he was telling the truth or not but he was of no more use to me.

The phone rang about five times before I eventually unplugged it from the wall.

Sahara

I called Chaz to hang out for the day.

"Hey cutie" I stated.

"What's up?" he replied dryly.

"You ok?"

"I'm good, what's up?"

"Nothing what's up with you? Why are you being so short?" I wondered.

"Because you hung up on me when I told you I couldn't give you what you wanted. And I called you all night but you ignored me."

"What are you talking about? I talked to you yesterday?"

"Yes, you forgot?" he asked.

"I'm sorry. I was tripping" I apologized, although I had no clue what he was talking about. I didn't want him to know my problem and that I was losing my mind.

I tried to remember my dream from last night to give me some kind of inkling of what may have happen but I couldn't. It was like that most times. Somedays I remembered bits and pieces of my dream (or should I say my other lives) and some days I didn't remember at all.

TWENTY-SEVEN

September 2005

Senior Year

Cleveland, Ohio

Nina

ONE THING FOR CERTAIN, TWO FOR SURE, I COULDN'T make any moves until I got this head of my done.

Driving down Miles to Best Beauty Stop, the hottest [not in a sense of decor or set up but in terms of having all the latest shit] hair store in Cleveland with the best deals.

India Arie's "Video" song played across my speaker on station 93.1 WZAK with Kym Sellers. I must have heard the song a million times but something resonated with me today that hadn't before.

The song felt like it had been set to slow motion like a chopped and screwed version. The lyrics soared out louder and louder and I started looking around as if someone had managed to sneak in my car with me unnoticed.

Damn I'm tripping I thought to myself! I ain't drunk, I ain't tired, I ain't been nowhere to have gotten slipped something.

I'm not the average girl from your video

My worth is not determined by the price of my clothes

No matter what I'm wearing I will always be

India Arie

When I look in the mirror and the only one there is me

Every freckle on my face is where it's supposed to be

And I know my creator didn't make no mistakes on me

My feet, my thighs, my Lips, my eyes, I'm loving what I see

I pulled up to hair store and parked behind the owner's car, a brand new black Range Rover, I'm assuming which parked perfectly in front of the entrance way. There were two of those orange cones an individual use to test drive in the front and rear of the truck.

In front of his SUV set an apple red 2005 Mercedes-Benz CLK320, drop top convertible.

I waited and watched to see who the cars belonged to. Ten minutes later an young African American female jumped in the Benz. I put the car in drive and decided to follow behind her.

She was average looking with an average body type. She wore bright red hair. Something about her spelled "stripper".

I was curious to see what kind of work she did or where she was living. I wanted to know what secret she knew that I didn't. I wanted to know what income could afford a convertible Benz.

But then I thought maybe she was loaning her dude's car. *But nah most dudes wouldn't want that kind of attention. That had to be her car!*

And sure enough, I followed her right down to the Alibi, a gentlemen's club in Downtown Cleveland.

I turned around and headed back to the beauty supply store. And just as I thought the parked SUV hadn't moved.

I went in the store and I stood around waiting for the clerk to assist me. While waiting, I watched 5 females purchase at minimum $100 worth of merchandise in the 20 minutes that I pranced around aimlessly.

Curiously, I pulled out my phone just to see the numbers from my head. 5 customers x $100 = $500. The store had made $500 in the time I had been there.

Assuming the same pattern continued every day during their regular business hours of 10 am - 10 pm;

60 minutes / 20 minutes = 3

5 customers x 3 = 15 customers per hour

15 customers x 12 hours (open business hours) = 180 customers a day

To be fair, let's say I came in on a rush and the average person spends $50.00 each visit on hair or beauty supplies as oppose to $100.00.

180 customers x $50 purchase = $9,000 in sales a day

Hell, I'd be pushing a $80, 000 car too.

I lost my appetite for the 4 packs of Italian body 18 inch Remy extensions I had come for.

I just settled with a couple of eyebrow shapers, some lip gloss and eye liner. I would rewash and re-wear some weave that I had stashed in my closet for a rainy desperate and low funds day.

That $400 looked real good in my pocket instead of theirs. I wasn't knocking their hustle though. They found a demand and provided the supply. I respect it.

But I wasn't falling for the trickery any longer. I had beautiful hair. I'll rock my own damn hair. Hell, most rich folks do. You don't get rich by giving all your damn money away.

Fuck a designer bag too. I'll rock some off-brand shit to have extra cash in my pocket. I'd rather have $2000 to do what I want with than have a $2000 bag and have nothing in it.

Screw a label. The way I seen it they had money already I was trying to get to where they were.

And I was about to get it!

Too many people spend money they haven't earned, to buy things they don't want, to impress people they don't like

-WILL SMITH

TWENTY-EIGHT

September 2005

Senior Year

Cleveland, Ohio

Sahara

THREE LETTERS NO ONE WANTS TO HEAR, H.I.V. THE NEWS came to my family all too hasty and unapologetically. Jason!

Of all people, why him? Well I guessed why anyone for that matter. But Jason was as lame as they came. He wasn't a fighter or a lover. He was silly, funny, caring and corny. True depiction of square.

I was positive Steve Irkle got more behind then Jason which confirmed the allegations that: "it only takes one time to catch it".

It made me question, *Was Jason paying the price for sins of our mother? Had God shown Violet mercy and taught her a lesson simultaneously.* Violet had been fortunate and blessed to dodge many of the consequences that usually accompanied such risky behavior.

With all the modern technology and improved drug regimens, individuals affected with the virus were living longer and healthier lives than when it first emerged in the 80's.

But unfortunately, Jason had been in denial about his status, noncompliant with his medications and his virus had transformed into acquired immunodeficiency syndrome better known as AIDS. And it was just a matter of time to his tragic demise.

He kept his disease from us all until he could no longer hide it. His body had begun to disintegrate.

He was thin, face sunken in and malnourished. The oral candidiasis, known to most as thrush murdered his appetite.

The process of coping for Jason and our family was an unsteady one. The process had a name, Kubler- Ross model or the five stages of grief/ death.

Kubler-Ross model

Denial- "it's not true?"

Anger- "why, it's not fair?"

Bargaining- "if I could turn back the hands of time, I would...."

Depression- "it's over, why go on?"

Acceptance – "it is what it is"

No one could put their head around why this was happening. It was a hard pill to swallow. My mother was crushed.

Just as we had learned this shocking truth, he was gone. My brother was dead!

TWENTY-NINE

October 2005

Senior Year

Cleveland, Ohio

Nina

AMATEUR NIGHT!!!!!

CALLING ALL THE LADIES TO

COME IN AND AUDITION

CASH PRIZES

THE SIGN READ OUTSIDE OF SWEET AS CANDY'S GENTLEMEN Club.

I contemplated whether to go in or not. I needed the money bad. My thirst for cash grew intensely. It was our last year of high school and on top of daddy needing a headstone, we needed to pay for senior dues, senior fees, prom, graduation and cap and gown photos.

While most of our classmates prepared for college, my mind was fixed on getting some money. Sahara wanted to go away to college but I couldn't foresee college until we first made it through our "now".

And Aniya was Aniya.

I decided to do it. I called all my girls down to come support me. Tiffany, Kia and my play sister: Tashia.

I told them to cheer like crazy and throw all the money they had at me and I'd give it back.

I assumed it couldn't be that hard to entice the crowd.

I first noted I had a talent in dancing on teen nights at Ken Ferguson and The Cotton Club. It was my practice grounds.

The DJs would close out the night with Adina Howard's, "T-shirt and Panties" and horny teenage boys would grab the nearest girl to get the last dance of the night.

I religiously left my practice toy excited and feenin' for more. I would leave them standing there trying to fix themselves.

By then, my eyes were set on much older prey who weren't so young, dumb and full of cum.

I even recalled further than that in middle school, when I was the only student in gym class who could climb the rope to the top of the ceiling.

A skill that would make climbing the pole a walk a park.

I reached the stage and my hands started to sweat and my feet wouldn't move. I was nervous until I realized forty people was looking at me and I would have rather been judged as a rookie dancer than a coward.

I told the DJ to play anything R. Kelly. And in less than 10 seconds "Butter Love" ran through the sounds system. I could feel the beat of the instruments on the floor of the stage.

My girls were screaming and cheering me on as requested.

I twirled around the pole a few times and pulled off my soft pink lace plunge teddy.

The crowd went wild. They didn't expect the newbie to go bare so quickly.

One guy stood up and from his seat that was approximately 4feet away, he threw a stack of what had to be $200 singles up at the ceiling.

The cash came trickling down all over me and the stage. I guess that's where the slang "making it rain" comes from.

My girls then followed suit. One after the other. Tashia threw twenty singles; Kia threw fifty singles and Tiffany slid two ten dollar bills in my thong strap.

I placed third in the audition of eleven contestants but the manager still offered me a job.

"When can you start," he asked?

"Now," I smiled.

"Alright. What's your name?" he asked.

I hadn't thought about a name. First thing I could think about was the fragrance I was wearing.

"Nina!" I smiled.

"N-I-N-A?" he asked as if there were 20 different ways to spell it.

"Yes!" I replied.

He added me to his roster. I scoped the room looking for Mr. 200 singles.

And he was nowhere to be found.

I gathered my friends, paid them back and made up a lie about me being pissed I didn't get 1st place and told them it was a bad idea that I considered dancing and that I was sorry for dragging them down there with me.

I convinced them to go on and leave without me. I insisted that I had to wait to collect my reward and I needed to be left alone to think.

THIRTY

October 2005

Senior Year

Maple Heights, Ohio

Sahara

IT'S FALL! A BEAUTIFUL DAY. AND I WAS LOVING IT! NOT TOO cold. Not too hot! And being a Cleveland native I appreciated a day like this day; Notorious for our winters and summers but most infamous for our unpredictable weather from day to day. It's 60 degrees at noon but it can easily deviate 25 degrees either direction with a blink of the eye by the evening.

I wish I could have said I was busy enjoying this beautiful day but instead I went to work at Sunshine Retirement Community. My nursing manager made me a deal I couldn't refuse, a 150 dollars bonus to come work evening shift, 3-11pm. There were always call-offs, especially on weekends, holidays and or second shift. If I was all about work and no play, I could have easily pulled in 64-72 hours a week.

Working as a STNA, had its pros and cons. A common pro was that it offered stability and job security. The world's population was aging rapidly. But the most pleasurable moments for me came from my patients' insight on life. I loved to hear my elders tell stories about their lives. Learning life's lessons through other's testimonies was truly captivating to me.

Even the most confused and disoriented human beings held on to some sort of recollection of their past. It amazed me watching my patients dancing and rehearsing popular tunes of their time during music hour. I fantasized about their thoughts.

A common con was the dealing with body fluids. If a person had a weak stomach the medical field wasn't the place to be. I had been pooped on, peed on, vomited on, bled on and spit at.

Not to mention, the worst con of being constantly disrespected and belittled. As a STNA, the disrespect came in all shapes, colors and sizes; family members of the patients, the patients themselves, nurses, administration and other interdisciplinary personnel.

But all and all, it was a job. Some days like any other profession was better or worse than other days.

On this day, my day started off as usual. I came in and took report from the STNA that I was relieving. I stood in on the nurses' report to listen for any acute changes with my residents since I had been off for a few days.

Nothing new was going on. Same ole same ole! Mrs. Johnson had been refusing her medicine all day. Mr. Lewis was complaining about dietary, his coffee was cold, he tired of eating the same bullshit, and he a grown ass man and they're giving him kid-size portions and so on and so on. Miss B doesn't like male caregivers so make sure that the male STNA on nights is switching her off with someone else. Mr. Walker's foot isn't improving so he probably will be getting am amputation soon. Mrs. Francis is still hanging on and she look like she may really go today or tomorrow for sure. She didn't eat or drink at all during day shift and her extremities have begun to mottle.

But let the nurses and doctor tell it, Mrs. Francis should have passed 2 years ago. Every other month, somebody is sure that her time is up but she'll fool them all and perk back up. She had been on hospice for as long as I had worked for the company and it's been months.

Mrs. Francis was one of those residents that were sweet as pie. She didn't bother a soul; a delight to have as a patient/resident.

But she was very noncompliant with her diet and health at home so her family admitted her to the facility because she needed someone to monitor her 24/7. She had Coronary Artery Disease, Hypertension, Diabetes, and COPD (Chronic Obstructive Pulmonary Disease).

Her family was extremely active with her care. One of her many children or grandchildren would visit the facility and assist the staff with her care daily.

But in the last few years, she had become fragile and weak. She had fallen so frequently that she was no longer ambulatory. And from there she gradually declined following her fall injuries. It seems as though when the elderly fracture their pelvis, hip or lower limb they are never the same.

After I listened to report, I did my rounds. I checked in on all my residents; checking to see that everyone was alive and well and that all my rooms and residents looked presentable.

I reached Mrs. Francis' room and as the nurse had previously stated she didn't look too good. I could always get her to crack a smile but not this day.

This day she wouldn't even open her eyes. She didn't move nor speak. I checked her vital signs and they were stable; 116/72 blood pressure, 84 pulse, 16 respirations, 97 degrees Fahrenheit, 93% pulse oximetry on 3 liters O2 via nasal cannula.

Just as I was exiting her room, I heard sobbing from her private connected bathroom. I hesitated before entering to see who it was but the caring, sensitive and compassionate side of me wouldn't allow me to mind my own business.

"Is everything okay", I asked through the closed door.

'She's dying, isn't she?" the woman cried. I opened the door. She was kneeling and hovering over the toilet as if she was vomiting.

"I can't make that call. I'm a STNA. Would you like me to get the nurse?"

"You bathe her, you change her, and you feed her! It's nothing she can tell me that you can't. Y'all are with her more than them!" She grew irritated, referring to the STNAs vs. the nurses.

"Nurses are better at explaining prognosis and other things. But I know what you mean. And I'm sorry, I didn't mean to say it like that" I apologized. "And also, God or whoever you worship has the last say. Who am I to make that call?"

"I'm asking you to" she stood up from the floor and faced me. Her mascara and eyeliner had run down her face. Her eyes were red and puffy from crying. She reeked of vomit. She was one relative I had never met before.

"I have never seen her like this before. She usually smiles when I call her name. She has never been a big breakfast eater for as long as I've known her but it is unusual for her to have skipped lunch as well. Her vitals are good. But honestly, she doesn't look well. I don't know!"

"Thank you", she whispered. I wasn't sure whether to leave her alone or stay with her for a few minutes more. I reached out and rubbed her shoulder. I wanted to say it would be okay but I hated when people said that to me. Before I could turn to leave she collapsed in my arms. I embraced her back.

She cried uncontrollably. I felt my shoulder getting wet. She sniffed and cried, attempting to contain the over pour of mucus. Her legs fell numb and I assisted her to the nearest chair in the room. Tears filled my eyes thinking about her situation.

I knew her pain. I had lived every minute of what she was going through. I didn't know who Mrs. Francis was to her and it really didn't matter. But what I did know was that she was important to her and she would miss her dearly once she was gone.

I thought back to the days that I didn't believe I could make it another minute of a day; days that I would have rather died than to cry another tear and wake up with that emptiness. Her life at that moment was all too familiar to me; first losing daddy, then Jason.

Since before I could remember I was preoccupied with persons' testimonies. I attentively listened and genuinely concerned myself with their life. Equally feeling their emotions as they spoke hurt, guilt, anger and other times pity.

Why some things made some individuals fold and others stronger, always seemed to fascinate me. I understood that everyone had to live their lives according to the way they see fit.

Everyone had a story to tell, while some may have been deeper than others everyone had a story behind their names that made them who they were.

I left her and Mrs. Francis alone but I peeped in on her hourly. And every time I checked in she was positioned in the same spot, seated with her head down in her hands on her lap.

THIRTY-ONE

October 2005

Senior Year

Maple Heights, Ohio

Aniya

SAHARA WAS ROUGH ON A CAR. SHE HAD ONLY HAD HER license and a car for nearly a year and she already needed brakes.

I drove to the nearest intersection and stumbled upon a Ford dealership. We had about had it with "backyard mechanics".

I elected to catch me a mister to give us free car tires or tires for a discounted price.

It wasn't hard to find something to wear in our closet. Nina, Sahara and I had the same style in clothing. But I was going for sexy this day.

I wore a white blazer as my top and bare breast, with skin tight ripped dark blue jeans and dark blue stiletto pumps. My itty-bitty B size breast were easily covered by the polyester fabric.

Nina had our belly pierced. I took out the basic stainless steel barbell that the tattoo parlor issues and I swapped it with a butterfly navel jewelry that hung just above my pants' button. Any lower and it would have definitely been caught in my clothing. But it gave the men something to stare at.

I had hoped that my catch was a young, full of energy and cute hunk. I needed tires and some action. I was well overdue for some penis.

I walked into the service department of the dealership and as I expected a room full of men was present.

I don't know whether my Sweet Pea body mist or low cut cleavage blazer had the room in a limbo but I was loving every minute of it.

"Hello," I snickered.

"Hi ma'am, can I help you," the funniest looking guy in the room had to answer.

"Yes, maybe. I need tires bad!" I replied.

"Oh, well I can help you with that" another guy replied, standing to my left. He came to save the day. The first guy was mad as hell he blocked his sale.

"Thank you!" I stated. Serviceman #2 wasn't the most attractive but something about him displayed charisma. His eyes sparkled when he talked. He had dimples and pearly white flawless teeth. And he was at least 6 foot.

"Do you know the brand of tire you want? Well lets first start with the make and model of your car. And the year?"

"Sunfire. Not sure the year. I can go out and check," I stated. "Now I'm on a budget. What's the least expensive tires you have?"

"Once you get me the year of the car, I'll promise to get you the best deal possible" He grinned.

I went out to the car to look for my insurance cards in the glove department. I felt someone following me. I turned around to see who it could be and it was a well-dressed middle aged man.

He looked to be too old to be courting me. He was well groomed with salt and pepper brush waves and a gold tee.

I turned back around and sat down on my passenger side seat to find my cards. He came and stood about a foot from my car hood.

"I just wanted to tell you how beautiful you are. You are so pretty to be dark-skinned! I usually don't like dark-skinned girls!" He stated.

I had heard that statement so much that it angered me. I despised being told I was "pretty to be dark-skinned". As to say, that every other shade is beautiful and being dark-skinned automatically disqualifies you. But for some extraordinary reason I was one of the "lucky few". I wanted to rip his ass a new hole. But I decided to see where he was going with it!

"Oh yea!" I replied.

"Yeah, you are astonishing!"

"Well thank you, I guess," I stated sarcastically.

"May I give you my number"

"Yeah only if you know someone who can give me a deal on 4 tires," I stated with a sassy attitude because I really didn't want to be bothered with his ass after his little comment.

"Bet! How about you go in there get what you need and I'll charge it to my card. And you let me take you to dinner tonight"

"So, what's the catch? What you want from me?" I asked with skepticism.

"Nothing just your time and attention."

"You don't want to sleep with me?' I asked, wanting to know if he would be a man and tell the truth.

"Well I only want what you're willing to give me. Of course, having sex with you will be fantastic but I want to get to know you too. All the sex in the world doesn't mean a thing if we can't hold a conversation."

Well played! I thought to myself. I found my cards, closed my door and walked beside him.

"Deal! But I don't even know you're name. My name is Sahara but call me Aniya." I stated.

"Emmanuel but I prefer Manny."

All new tires, dinner date and some D out the deal. I was winning!

The blacker the berry the sweeter the juice

-WALLACE THURMAN

THIRTY-TWO

April 2006

Senior Year

Cleveland, Ohio

Nina

I HAD BEEN WORKING AT THE CLUB FOR SEVERAL MONTHS and I was making a decent living. I had developed a spending habit. As fast as the money came it had gone.

I found a respect for street hustlers. They were willing to do what they had to do to get the things they needed and wanted.

Surprisingly though, I had managed to keep it away from Sahara. I was careful about coming home at a decent hour during the week to allow her time to sleep and be prepared for school in the morning.

I hid my exotic costumes and shoes in a duffle bag under the trunk floor in the spare tire compartment. And she never went in there.

And I only spent money on her pay days. I hid the extra money all around our apartment.

I felt like a drug dealer.

THIRTY-THREE

April 2006

High school

Senior Year

Sahara

IT WAS ALMOST TIME FOR GRADUATION. I WOULD SOON have been "officially a grown ass woman". I had turned 18 in December but it still didn't feel like much.

I couldn't wait to walk across that stage. I earned it. With all the hell, I had been through over the years it was good to finally be rewarded.

I knew my dad and brother would have been proud of me.

I wanted to go to college but I couldn't seem to get accepted to any universities or colleges I preferred.

Both times I was supposed to take my ACT, I was hungover but like always I didn't remember drinking. The first time I went to take my exam I couldn't hardly finish it. I had a throbbing headache and I vomited all over my clothes and the desk, attempting to run to the wastebasket.

The second time, I completely overslept and missed it.

I assumed it may have been the wrong time in my life to go away for school. I would work and save until the time was right.

Nina

Oops… I didn't intend for her to be hungover for her ACTs. Why did they have to test on Saturdays anyways? I couldn't afford to miss making my money on Friday nights. And I needed liquor to get me in the mood.

I don't know why Sahara had the idea of college. There's nothing for us there. I raided the apartment and trashed any and all college pamphlets and brochures. We needed money and I was going to get it for us.

The day was dragging and Mr. Watson was out sick for the day. Our regular substitute teacher, Mr. O'Malley was filling in for him. I usually tried to lay low when he was on duty.

I had dreams about Mr. O'Malley. We had become acquaintances. And he always gave me that awkward creepy stare.

"Sahara, you should really get more sleep at night and not during my class," Mr. O'Malley stated. I woke up to a gentle tap on my shoulder. I had drifted off to sleep that fast. "Would you see me after class, please?"

I nodded yes.

Bells ring. I gathered my things and headed to the teacher's desk. He waited until the last student had exited the class before speaking.

"Did you work last night" he asked?

"Yeah"

"I didn't see you. I was there."

"I worked," I answered. Wondering to myself, *why he would be at the nursing home?*

"Where at", he asked curiously?

"Are we done here? I really need to go," I walked a few feet closer to the door.

"Well I hope to see you this evening. And try to stay up during class. If I cut you slack, I'll have to cut everyone some slack," he smirked, winked and extended his arms for a hug.

I ignored his gesture and turned to walked out the class.

I couldn't believe he had the audacity to patronize me. And then wanted to feel me up. *Pervert!*

THIRTY-FOUR

April 2006

Senior Year

Cleveland, Ohio

Sahara

IF I HAD A DOLLAR FOR EVERY TIME I SEEN A GOOD GIRL FALL for a bad boy, including myself, I would be a millionaire. Why opposites attract is the darnest thing.

I fell for Rich at first sight. I knew he was a bad boy instantly. But he was so damn fine.

I had no certainty what exactly it was that Rich did for a living, most likely something illegal but I loved the way he made me feel. He was my weakness.

Rich was 27 years old. 6'4 olive skin tone, perfect Colgate smile, athletic built about 175/180 pounds with bow legs. He wore fresh crisp Allen Iverson styled braids with a clean line up.

He would have been to pretty for me had it not been for the old scar beneath his right eye 3"L x 1"W. That I later came to learn that was from an after-club brawl and being hit in the face with a crow bar.

He was a perfect ensemble of thug and sex symbol. He had a meat package every woman would dream for. Ten inches and thick to say the least. And his mouth game was everything to write home about as well.

Sadly, he was a male whore. He had a woman for every day of the week. But I loved the ground he walked on. Because of his finesse, sense of humor, sex and looks of course, his suspicious lifestyle and street credit.

Rich carried a pistol in reach at all times; three or more in his house, two in his car and one on his person. He knew everybody and everybody knew him and his 4 older brothers. Not positive whether he was that loved or that feared.

THIRTY-FIVE

July 2006

Post-Graduation

Cleveland, Ohio

Nina

I WASN'T A FAN OF ANIYA AT FIRST. BUT WHEN SHE KNOCKED off an assistant NFL coach, Manny she was due her props.

At first, I thought like everybody else, coochie was coochie. That's until I met Manny. He showed me things I had never seen. He taught me things I had never been taught. I owed him for the woman he made.

Some girls learn that it takes more than their behind to bring to the table while I learned the right behind delivered the right way to the right man is most times the only necessity to bring to the table.

The *freaky one* was going to cut him loose until I intervened.

He refurnished our entire apartment for our graduation present; introduced us to 5 star restaurants out of state, first class air travel and true chivalry. In the few months of us dating I had been to more states than I had in all my life combined.

Edible arrangements delivered to our apartment just because it was Tuesday; bouquet of pink roses delivered to Sahara's job because they're our favorite; and he had me thinking "Beautiful" was our name.

We were treated to weekly spa pampering; Mani, Pedi, facials, Brazilian wax, hot stone massages, the works. Weekend rendezvous at Poconos Resort, Kalahari or a getaway cabin.

Manny was strapped with cash. And he liked me a lot or should I say **Her**. But the *boogie one*, Sahara was too head over hills for Rich. *If she would've let me lead we would've been alright.*

THIRTY-SIX

July 2006

Sweet As Candy's

Cleveland, Ohio

Nina

THE NIGHT WAS WINDING DOWN AND I FOUND MYSELF trying to rush to the dressing room unnoticed. I often did every night to avoid the persistent men who would stay until close to lure dancers home or to a hotel with them.

I prided myself for not being or becoming that girl who did whatever if the price was right. I by no means judged the next woman for what she did but I knew I didn't want any parts of that slippery slope.

I felt that for me it would be a road of self-destruction. "Stand for something or fall for anything" was something I reminded myself every night. As tempting and challenging it would be sometimes to say 'NO" and go home; I knew I had to.

Money was like a drug. The more I had, the more I wanted and I knew I couldn't start something I knew I wouldn't be able to stop. The disease of "more". Never feeling satiety.

Not to mention, I knew my life at the club was short lived and didn't want to do anything that could potentially jeopardize our future or tarnish our name. I knew we would one day be able to recover for having once been an exotic dancer but I didn't think we could ever recover from being a prostitute. That label is tough to dilute.

I couldn't believe I let scandalous ass Reese, a seasoned exotic dancer talk me into considering doing a private party for this alleged money couple. This guy, Scotty was supposed to be loaded and wanted to give his bisexual girl a private party for her birthday.

Scotty was an ex heroin dealer and Shay was a booster from Morris Black projects. Shay could get you anything from baby clothes to authentic Gucci shit from Saks.

As crooked as they both were and could have been they both were known to bless the city. Shay would donate stolen goods every holiday to the battered women and children shelters. Scotty would coach and mentor kids in the summer and winter months for Muny League football.

Reese seen me headed for the door and she stopped me.

"Hey boo," Reese yelled out to me.

"What's up Hun?" I asked, as I walked towards Reese who was sitting at the bar.

"I know you don't be into private stuff but I got something you may be down with," Reese smirked.

I gazed at her with curiosity and skepticism.

"So, you know Scotty. Ole boy that come thru every other day or so throwing money on the whole team and popping Moey (a term many used for drinking Moet Champagne). He wants to have a little private set for him and wifey at his place. He wants you to come with me but he was sure you would say no if he had asked"

"What he want, you know I ain't down with that other...."

"I know, I know, I know," Reese replied cutting me off in mid-sentence. "He just wants us to dance for an hour or two and then we out"

"How much and when? I got class Tuesdays and Thursdays. So, Mondays' and Wednesdays' nights are out too," I lied hoping she was going to say one of the forbidden days.

"That's cool. This Friday or Saturday. Let me know."

"How much?" I grew irritated thinking Reese was avoiding my question.

"Now you know he got it," Reese looked at me as if I was asking a stupid question.

"Reese, I need to know before I say yes or no and I need my bread walking in the door not a moment after!" I knew then that it was some bullcrap involved. *Why was she taking so long to run it down to me*, I thought to myself?

"Five hundred a piece for sure but I may be able to get us more. And you know he like to stunt. So, he may still make it rain while we dancing. So, for real we may leave with a good 750 each. So, you with me?"

"Let me think on it for a night. I'll let you know tomorrow night"

"Don't miss this boat! Easy, easy come up!" Reese persuaded.

"I gotcha!"

I headed for the door. I went to my car and drove off thinking about Reese's proposal. All of my bills were paid up for the next 3 months. But I still needed $200 to buy dad's headstone. I knew I could make this money without even doing the party but I wanted to get my dad's headstone ASAP.

Daddy had been deceased for three years and I had promised myself that he would have had a headstone by this birthday which had already passed. I needed to have had Daddy's headstone paid in full by October or I would have had to wait until April to have the stone plotted due to Ohio weather elements.

I decided. I would do the party.

THIRTY-SEVEN

July 2006

Sweet As Candy's
Cleveland, Ohio

Nina

IT WAS HILARIOUS WATCHING SOME OF THE GIRLS AT THE end of the night scatter like home pest when the lights came on. Those black lights were some bad motha suckas. They were good at hiding the boogieman.

I would get a kick out of guys drooling over a couple dancers and imagining if they had only seen what I had seen would they still be as mesmerized.

But then again, "the power of the pu$$y" wasn't nothing to be played with either. *Who knows*, I thought! They may have had that platinum package!

The club had its main roster but guest dancers from other local clubs would frequent the club on popular nights: Wet and Wild Wednesday, Fridays and Saturdays. Most nights it would be 12-16 dancers working.

Missy was my favorite. She taught me the game. She gave me the contact information to the seamstress who designed and sold the girls' custom outfits. Missy was a beautiful dark chocolate complexion with dimples. She was southern style thick with a wash board tummy. Considered overweight in the eyes of BMI standards but perfect for men who love a little extra to hold on to. Huge butt!

A lot of girls would say they really didn't have to work but most knew better who knew them. Missy was one of the million who truly didn't have to dance. I believed she danced in some weird way to keep her man in line. Showing him that other men wanted her just as bad I guessed.

Her dude was probably 20 years her senior and word around was that he was a retired Air Force Colonial and was some big shot at the Federal building. He accompanied her every night to the club and every time she took the stage he would bless her with a tsunami of singles. And if she was friends with a fellow dancer she would let him bless them too but of course not on the scale of her. And she dared anyone to try to sneak and talk to him, it would have been hell to pay. She had no problem fighting over him.

Star was a straight hustler. She knew how to work the entire crowd. She was bisexual. She made her money from both women and men. She also sold marijuana. She was a ripe banana complexion and mid height. She had small breast and an even smaller waist with a heavy bottom. Her hips and butt looked like they belonged on another body. Star had a pole routine that commanded everyone's attention.

Ariel was the sexiest dancer there. She was pretty cold at dancing too. She took her name from her favorite Disney princess, Little Mermaid. Best body award went to her hands down but she had no clue. She had the confidence the size of a pea. She never made direct eye contact with her audience. Facially, she was average looking, butterscotch skin tone but built like a coco cola body similar to Kim Kardashian but all natural.

Destiny was the owner's girlfriend and also the "house mom". She was responsible for "managing" the dancers. She was the prettiest girl at the club (which explained why she was the owner's main squeeze) put you in mind of Halle Berry. And she could dance to anything; R&B, Hip Hop, Alternative Rock or Pop. But her body didn't measure up to her face. She was average built. Almond skin tone. Her body displayed all the signs of a woman that bear child(ren). Her abdomen and breast sagged and were untoned. Her lower abdomen wore striae 4 shades deeper than her skin tone.

Pebbles was fortyish, the oldest of all the girls, the veteran. She had been there long as the doors had been open. She was also a bully and most was afraid of her. She would almost intimidate men to get them to buy a dance. And she kept drama going amongst the dancers and bar staff. She was caramel complexion, mediocre looking with an average body type with a few extra pounds.

Sunny was the nicest of all the girls. She kept to herself. She was biracial and really fair skinned. She wore a ton of make up to conceal her acne and blemishes but when she was done her skin was flawless. She could have been a paid MAC cosmetics model. Sunny was very thin (like size 4) and petite frame. Came to get her money and went home.

Reese was the snake of the bunch. She couldn't be trusted no further than she was thrown. She would rob, kill or steal for cash. She put me in mind of Gabrielle Union. Very pretty! She could have been mistaken for being Gabby's baby sister; exact same features, complexion and body type.

Alexis was the sexual free spirit and little mentally off. She had no type whatsoever. If the price was right, she slept with young, old, black, white, Latino, Asian, woman, man, gay and straight. No preference. She was a cute girl with a baby face; look like she wasn't a day over 16. Alexis was tall, thin, fair skinned tone with huge 34 E size bra breast.

Sweetie was the gossiper and two-faced dancer of the crew. She was nice on the surface but I have always been leery of the female that's extra cool with everybody. Sweetie had a really nice body too. Not as nice as Ariel but she was definitely the runner up.

She had face abnormalities as if she may have suffered from a mild case of Down syndrome or FAS (Fetal Alcohol Syndrome). I assumed that's why she tried to befriend everyone to avoid malicious criticism.

Tokyo was the most unique of us all. She was well known for her body art extremes. 80% of her body was covered with tattoos. She wore micro dermal implants on her cheek bones and sternum. She was laced with piercings: complete lobes and helix, both tragus, nipples, tongue, septum and clitoris.

She had a Miami edition of the "mommy make over", a Brazilian butt lift with liposuction and fat transfer, tummy tuck and breast augmentation. The perfect constructed body. She was a bad sistah but a little odd.

THIRTY-EIGHT

August 2006

Sunny Slope Estates

Maple Heights, Ohio

Sahara

LIVING ON MY OWN WAS LIBERATING BUT BORING. I MISSED my grandparents subconsciously. I still went by to visit them monthly, on my off days.

And aside from dating a ladies' man, I was often lonely. Daddy and Jason had passed away. My mother was in rehab. Tashia was expecting another daughter. And Tiffany had recently birthed twin boys.

Chaz had moved on from our high school puppy love and was engaged. Kia was soon leaving me to go away to college at Florida A&M University to study Forensic Science.

I was all by myself. I was casually dating but I wasn't really interested.

Since graduating, my life consisted of working, sleeping and dreaming.

My other lives of what I could envision was more lively, entertaining and interesting than mine.

I longed for a true companion and not a part time lover.

Your attitude determines your altitude

-ZIG ZIGLAR

THIRTY-NINE

August 2006

Cleveland, Ohio

Aniya

AND THEN THERE WAS DRU. HE HAD A HEART OF GOLD, confidence of a billionaire guru and a sense of humor to make a Grinch smile. But unfortunately, he wore a face only a mother would love. My being shallow could have easily overcast his qualities. He was one of the best people I was fortunate to have met coming into adulthood.

Our first date was priceless. We drove 45 minutes outside of town to Pickle Bills Lobster House for all you can eat crab legs. Once we arrived he excused himself to the bathroom and after about 10 minutes he exited the bathroom to tell me that he had an emergency and had to get back to Cleveland. He didn't elaborate and I didn't want to pry. He dropped me off to my car and we went our separate ways.

After a few months of dating he decided to share with me the events of that evening.

"You know when we first met and I took you out to eat; and we left as soon as we got there?"

"Yeah, how could I forget. I didn't get my damn crab legs," I laughed.

"Aye…I took a shit in their bathroom. My dumb ass ate a darn cookie and cream ice cream cone knowing I'm lactose intolerant. There wasn't one roll of tissue or paper towel in that damn bathroom. I was too embarrassed to come out and ask the staff in front of you. I had to go home, with an itchy butt and wash my ass"

I laughed hysterical visualizing his story. "You couldn't hold it"?

"Hell nah, have you ever tried to hold your shit? It doesn't feel good," He confessed.

We both laughed so hard we cried just at the thought of it.

Dru was notorious for outlandish behavior. This crazy dude would even mark his underwear and clothes with his initials in hopes of catching the perpetrator in his apartment complex who had been stealing his clothing.

I laughed every single time I seen his 35plus grown behind with his name in his boxer briefs like some darn preschooler.

But what was even funnier is that he was dead serious. He swore his trap would catch his villain.

The sight made my day every time.

Dru was a true woman pleaser and adventurer. And I almost forgot the most important quality: a freak!

If I was into the whole marriage thing, he would have been a potential prospect.

We would visit museums, go see plays, watch the sunset at the lake, go fishing, hiking and rock climbing.

He also took me on my first motorcycle bike ride. I was terrified but he swore to only go 25 mph while I was riding.

He found something new and fun for us to do almost every week. And afterwards he would treat himself to an ALL YOU CAN EAT walking Hershey Kiss. I loved to take his tongue bath.

FORTY

August 2006

Scotty's Residence

Shaker Heights, Ohio

Nina

REESE AND I ARRIVED IN SEPARATE VEHICLES TO SCOTTY and Shay's home near Lee Road and Chagrin Blvd. Shay greeted the both of us at the door with a bottle of Hennessey in one hand and a bottle of Absolut Vodka in the other hand.

"Hey y'all! I'm ready to see some ass. Oh, y'all gave me a selection. I got a red bone and a chocolate bunny. I hope y'all drinking 'cus I can't drink all this alone." Shay announced.

"Yes ma'am," I smirked. I usually drank Grey Goose vodka. But I figured a couple of shots couldn't hurt. Reese didn't drink. She rolled up a blunt to relax her instead.

"So, none for you, Reese," Shay stated! "Well more for us," she giggled.

Shay already appeared intoxicated and it was early in the afternoon. Her eyes were glossy, she was laughing at almost everything and she had an unsteady gait.

I began listening and looking out for Scotty. I had heard other dancer's warnings about doing private parties and not being paid after having danced all night.

I wouldn't get comfortable until he came through on our agreement. Reese and I stood in the living area waiting for directions. There sat a three-piece black leather sectional, 50/60 in TV, an entertainment center with hundreds of movies and CDs, black glass and wood coffee tables, and a host of family photos

"Y'all can go to the back room on the right to get changed," Shay pointed up the steps to their bedroom. Reese proceeded to walk towards the room but I stood in place.

"What, you waiting on Scotty? He'll be back. He stepped out for a few," Shay noticed my hesitation.

I instantly grew impatient. *He knew that we were coming*, I thought. *See I should have gone with my first mind and stayed my butt home. I'll get dress in my outfit but I will not dance until I have my cash in my hand.*

"Alright, would you have him come back here," I followed Reese towards the bedroom.

Scotty and Shay's room was practically empty. There was a King Cherry Wood Sleigh bed, a 26/32 inch TV mounted on the wall, mirror ceiling and a ceiling height stainless steel dancer's pole which was mounted one foot from their bed. It was obvious that this couple was very kinky and outgoing with their sexuality.

Ten minutes had gone by and I was applying my makeup when Scotty walked in.

"You thought I was on some trash baby girl. I wouldn't play with you about no money." Scotty handed Reese and I five $100 bills a piece. "Alright y'all hurry up before my girl get too drunk and don't know what's going on."

He exited the room.

"Hey, can you do me a favor," I whispered to Reese after I was certain Scotty was gone. "I don't want them thinking we doing anything else besides dancing please don't do that other stuff you do today or if you do let me leave first."

"You need to get off of that goody two shoes shit and know when to get this bread," Reese stood from the bed and walked out the room. She left the door open behind her. "Come on!"

I finished applying my mascara and lip gloss and walked behind Reese. By time I came downstairs, Reese was sitting on Scotty lap smoking her blunt.

I walked next to Shay and stuck out my hand for a shot glass. I took four shots of vodka one right after another to add to the half pint of Grey Goose I consumed on the drive to their house.

"Put on some music," Scotty yelled out to Shay. Shay shuffled through their CD collection. She inserted three CDs into their CD player. First song to play was Silks' "There's a Meeting in my Bedroom" and next up was H-Town "Knockin' the Boots". And I felt right at home. 90s R&B was my music genre preference.

I stood in the center of the living room and began to slow wind. I rolled my hips while holding my right breast with one hand and pretending to bite at my nipple and imitating masturbating through my thong with my left hand.

Reese began to give Scotty a lap dance and grope on Shay (who sat beside them) breast all at once. I hated she had got to Scotty first. I didn't want to dance for Shay.

Afraid that I was being too distant, I walked closer to Shay and stood in between her legs.

Shay started kissing my stomach as I rolled my hips in front of her. I turned my back to Shay to distract her from kissing on me. I bend over to hold my ankles while I performed a skill many dancers performed. I contracted and relaxed my vaginal muscles. This would in turn make the fabric of my thong move in and out.

Most observers would be in "aww" witnessing a woman's physical control over this sacred area. As expected, Shay was thrilled. She started tapping Scotty to watch too.

This made Reese jealous. Reese started to grope Scotty genitals to regain his attention.

I was irritated. I had Shay right where I wanted her and then Reese was wheeling her back. Shay leaned forward and kissed each of my butt cheeks. In attempts to distract Shay once more, I set down on her lap. I rolled my hips and played with my breast.

Shay was ready for more satisfaction. She leaned over and pull the string loose to Reese's bikini thong. Reese followed up by untying the opposite side.

Reese laid down on the floor now bottomless with her legs widely separated. She pulled anal beads from her vagina and then reinserted them into her anus.

Shay lifted me from her lap and crawled on the floor next to Reese. Shay played with the beads in Reese's anus; Reese squirmed and moaned for about 2 minutes until she had an orgasm.

Scotty was in heaven. He threw dollar bills in the air, landing all over Reese.

Once Reese regained composure, she gathered her money up. She then ripped off Shay's dress and placed herself and Shay in a 69 position. They both competed at pleasing each other to see who would cum the fastest.

I couldn't deny that the sight had me horny which was a hard thing to do. But I stood my ground, I could see Scotty watching me in my peripheral vision.

Shay paused their session. She stood and lead Reese by the hand upstairs to she and Scotty's bedroom.

I glanced over at Scotty confused on what to do or say proceeding Reese and Shay's foreplay. He broke the silence.

"You don't have to do anything you don't want to do. We can sit and talk if you want."

I smiled, relieved that I had dodged that bullet.

"What you in school for," He asked. Everyone at the club thought I was in my twenties and had assumed I was already in college.

"I'm just taking some general education requirements now." I lied.

"You're not sure what you want to do?"

"Nope," I replied. "How about you, what you do for a living?"

"A little of this and a little of that. I ran it up when I was out here slanging, now I'm retired and living." He smirked.

"Must be nice."

Reese returned to the living room alone, fully dressed and with her belongings.

I guess Scotty had sensed something was strange.

"Leaving so soon?" He asked

He grabbed Reese by her waist and lead her back up the steps. I set like a duck waiting to put together what was going on. I heard Scotty laugh and a door slam.

"You really thought you were just going to leave too," he said. Seconds later, I heard commotion and seen Reese tumbling down the steps.

Fearing she may have been hurt I ran to her side to see if she was alright. I helped her stand to her feet and Scotty came from nowhere and back handed Reese back down to the floor. Before she could stand from the fall, he had his foot in her chest.

"Bitch I could kill you right now and no one would know. Who the fuck would miss your trifling ass? You a greedy bitch $800 wasn't enough for your scandalous ass, huhn?"

He pulled his gun, a 9-millimeter silver automatic from his back waist band. I attempted to run for the door and he yelled out to me!

"Sit yo ass down," he said, pointing the gun at my face.

I knew I was as good as dead too. Guilty by association. I remembered back to the day Aniya had a gun pulled on her and we managed to escape without a scratch. But I knew Scotty was more skilled and wise; and getting away may not be that feasible for us this day.

I took a seat on the couch in fear of what was next.

Reese lied on the floor in a fetal position, shielding her face with her arm. Scotty stood over her in rage. He demanded Reese to her knees. He unzipped his blue jeans. And his jeans and boxers fell to his calves. And I presumed that we both would most likely be raped and murdered.

"You better suck my dick like your life depends on it because it does. And bitch you better not bite me or I will kill your ass fa sho!" Scotty demanded, reaching down, grabbing Reese by her hair and pulling her head up to his perianal area.

Reese performed oral sex on Scotty as her life did depend on it. Right as Scotty climaxed he forcefully grabbed the back of Reese head and pushing every inch of his size 9 wide into her mouth. Audible gagging could be heard.

"And don't make no mess. Swallow it all," he instructed.

I must have prayed a thousand times that this horrendous evening had come to end.

She gave him what he wanted. There is no reason for him to keep us, I thought to myself.

Scotty released his gripped from Reese neck. Reese stood to her feet and attempted to collect her things. She hadn't said a word.

"What you think that's it? You ain't done!" He stared Reese down.

He removed his pants and boxer briefs from his legs and set back on the sectional. "Nina pour me a drink. And get her and you one too!" I obeyed.

Scotty took a sip and I threw a shot back. Reese guzzled her double shot down in seconds. I had never seen Reese touch a drink. But she was drinking this day. This was confirmation of her terror.

"Give her that $800," Scotty said to Reese. He pointed at me.

Reese reached in her bra and handed me her $800 without a question. "See what happens when you're a scandalous thirsty bitch! You ended up dogged, lonely and broke!"

"You ready, 'cus he is," he pointed down to his erected penis.

Reese lowered to her knees and crawled over to Scotty. She hand stroked his penis before she licked his tipped. Scotty was passionately moaning with his arms folded behind his head and looking down at Reese.

"Nina, you're free to go! Stay in school! Don't end up like this bitch," he stared down at Reese!

I went to the bedroom for my things. Shay was laid out across the bed, completely naked with her legs spread and laying in a puddle of vaginal secretions.

I didn't bother getting dressed. I made a dash for the door before Scotty could change his mind. Last I seen was Reese's head in Scotty lap and completing her punishment.

FORTY-ONE

September 2006

Sunny Slope Estates

Maple Heights, Ohio

Sahara

I DAY DREAMED, I WALKED INTO FAMILY FIRST Monuments and bought daddy a headstone; One of the nice ones with a big photo of him. I paid cash for it in full: $1,397.54.

I don't know how I did it. But it's a relief.

I played scavenger hunt around the apartment looking for a receipt of purchase or buyer's agreement. I couldn't find one anywhere.

Next week, when I'm off work I'm going to see for myself.

It can't be real!

FORTY-TWO

September 2006

Sunny Slope Estates

Maple Heights, Ohio

Nina

I RETURNED TO THE CLUB NEVER TO SEE REESE AGAIN. I prayed for her safety but was hopeful when I hadn't seen or heard of a missing woman.

We had reframed from watching the news and most popular TV crime series shows. Hearing the repeated violence and abuse of people especially children, even if it was fictional, left a bad taste in our mouth.

But I made an exception and tuned in; paying close attention for several weeks to channel 19 news and the Plain Dealer, Cleveland's newspaper following the incident.

I didn't know what exactly Reese had stolen but I didn't believe anything could have been worth the humiliation and degradation she had faced.

Scotty had scarred me for life. We couldn't go on dates with any man without me thinking about that night at his home with Reese.

I started protecting us in the event that a man would plan our abduction, rape, torture and or murder. I would write a guy's name, phone number, license plate number and general physical description on a note pad at our place and leave it plain sight.

I would call my close friends, Kia and Tiffany and let them know also.

I would leave some trace of DNA on the guy's person or possessions. Sometimes, I would comb or brush my hair in their car to leave back shed hair.

Other times, I would pretend to rub a man's head to get his scalp cells beneath my nails. Or I would scrape the skin cells of our inner cheeks with my finger and rub my finger somewhere on the interior of his car.

I made sure I touched every surface I could to leave our finger prints behind. *No one would ever assault me and get away with it*, I vowed!

I needed a weapon and there was one person I knew who could get me one.

"Hey babe," I called Sahara's lover.

"What's up chocolate," Rich answered.

"I know I told you I would never do any parties but I let this girl talk me into it. I thought it would be safe because I was going with her and we were hired by a couple."

"Who were they?" He asked.

"Some dude Scotty and his wife Shay," I replied.

"What happened?"

"Ok, when we made it to their home things was cool up until Reese tried to pull a fast one and take the chick in the bedroom and stole some money I think from the guy. I mean he had already given us 500 each."

"How much she take?" He asked.

"I don't know what she took or how much but it must've been a lot. He pulled a gun out on us both. And he made her give him head. I thought he was going to rape and kill us both. I guess he knew I didn't have anything to do with it 'cus I was downstairs and she was up; and she came out with all her clothes walking fast to the door. She was going to leave me there if he hadn't stopped her."

"Man, why the hell would you do that? You didn't know that dude. And you have a job and work the club. You didn't need that punk ass 500. I would've gave it to you if I knew you were that pressed for cash." He was obviously upset with my actions.

"I know, I know, I wasn't thinking. But that was a first and last for me. Trust!" I reassured him. "But I wanted to know if you can get me a piece?"

"A gun? I'm not giving you no damn gun!" He laughed.

"Alright well I'll call you later!"

"Hey can I get some of that *good shit* later," he asked!

I hung up the phone. I'll let Sahara deal with him later if she wants to.

FORTY-THREE

October 2006

Sunny Slope Estates

Maple Heights, Ohio

Sahara

I RESTED IN THE HOUSE FOR THE LAST FEW DAYS. I TOOK A shower and got ready to start my day. I went out to my car and noticed the headlights were left on. My battery was dead.

I hadn't experienced a battery dying before. But I remembered the car salesman telling me that there was an emergency kit in the trunk. When I popped the trunk, I seen a pink gym bag. I opened the bag to find a pair of two-inch platform, 6-inch heel, red patent leather laced-up calf length boots; a school girl costume, custom bedazzled bikinis with matching garter belts, a pager and a box of business cards.

The business card displayed a photo of me dressed in a swim suit and a short length wig. It read:

NINA

Available for parties, hosting and urban modeling

I called the number listed in the far-right corner of the card. A sequence of tones rang out. I entered my cell number and hit the # key to submit the page. The pager in the bag sounded off.

Those were in fact my items. I was a stripper... *but when, where, how, why?*

That explains the extra money and muscle aches. Disgusted, I went back to my apartment to send for roadside assistance, AAA.

Nina

Damn...

FORTY-FOUR

Two hours later...

Sahara

I WATCHED MY TV SCREEN IN A TRANCE. ONE OF MY MANY favorite movies, Sister Act II was airing on Lifetime. I listened to Delores played by Whoopi Goldberg and felt her speaking to me.

I went to my mother who gave me this book called Letters to a Young Poet. Rainer Maria Rilke. He's a fabulous writer. A fellow used to write to him and say: "I want to be a writer. Please read my stuff." And Rilke says to this guy: "don't ask me about being a writer. If when you wake up, you can think of nothing but writing… than you're a writer."

I stood up from the couch and left my place to go on a walk. I walked for hours. A million and one things were rolling through my head.

I came home to retrieve my car.

I drove two and a half hours to register for classes at the University of Toledo. I planned to attend that Spring '07, majoring in English with a concentration in Creative Writing.

I was already behind. My peers were completing fall semester and I would just be getting started.

It was a spare of the moment decision that I deemed critical for my life. I couldn't sit back and destroy myself before I had the chance to try to advance and better myself.

I needed a change. I needed a fair shot. I needed redemption!

Aniya

College is fine by me. They'll be plenty of fish in the sea for me!

Nina

She can move but I'm always going to locate that paper! Detroit here I come.

A man without vision shall perish

-PROVERBS 29:18

FORTY-FIVE

October 2006

Sweet As Candy

Cleveland, Ohio

Nina

I HAVE MORALS DESPITE WHAT MS. BOOJIE MAY THINK. I respected her life, our life too much to just do "anything". I prevented us from getting expelled years ago. Why would I hurt our future now?

I set back and observed the girls I worked with and the females that made the most money were willing to do whatever to get their money.

And I was tempted at times. But I thought, *well how long will that last and was that even important*? Should I get it like everyone else while I could get it? Would people see us as different because I had boundaries and several did not? Or would we all still be placed in one box as "strippers"!

Somewhere between wanting to go all in to maximize my earnings and thinking about our name and legacy, I decided that her (our) character and principles which she (we) lived by meant more.

She wanted to be a writer and I would never knowingly sabotage her. She gave me no credit at all. I was about my money without a doubt. And I could be a little risky at times but I wasn't Aniya. She needed checking not me.

I recall riding the Greyhound all the way to Atlanta, 18 and a half hours exactly just to turn right back around after refusing to sleep with my connect at Magic City, the popular gentlemen club and celebrity hang out.

Sahara can't blame her shortcomings on me!

FORTY-SIX

February 2007

University of Toledo

Toledo, Ohio

Aniya

I HAD CUT OFF ALMOST ALL MY FELLOWS BACK HOME. I TRIED the distant relationships for a few weeks but it became old fast.

I met a couple guys on and off campus that wasn't really my type but they were satisfactory for the time being.

Nina found some local gigs and where she went, I always followed. Catching a guy who can lay down the pipe and had ends was always a plus.

Nina would have the money. I'll take the sex.

And… Sahara could have the love. It all worked out!

FORTY-SEVEN

February 2007

All Starz

Detroit, Michigan

Nina

I FOUND MY WAY AROUND THE D PRETTY WELL CONSIDERing I had never been there before and didn't know anyone. I was eager to see what the Motor City had to offer.

From what I heard it was infested with drugs and crime similar to Cleveland but for a dancer where there's drugs there's money. So, the gentlemen's clubs were banging. Detroit had a reputation for housing the cornbread thick girls like Serena Williams; and the girls who weren't naturally gifted could purchase their dream body for the right price.

But I on the other hand was hoping to be the needle in the haystack. A slim, thick in all the right places, Hershey Kisses for the men who dared to be different.

I had never seen so much cash before in my life.

I mean daddy had spoiled me rotten. So, I was accustomed to money and nice things. But this was different.

My hands grew exhausted from counting so much money. Carpel tunnel at its worst! I could have asked for help but I didn't trust those D girls.

They were cut throat. I had heard countless treacherous stories of girls setting up their colleagues after witnessing their earnings for the night.

I threw the uncounted money in my bag. I planned to go to the bank that morning.

I finally had experienced the tsunami effect. Cleveland dope boys rarely blessed me like that but the Detroit dope boys showed love.

I usually attracted the more mature subtle reserved men probably due to my song selection.

I'm an authentic Soul and R&B kind of girl. When R. Kelly - "Slow Dance", Chris Bender- "Who Will I Choose", Xscape- "Do You Want To" or Kut Klose – "I like", would start to play I and everyone else knew it was my time to enter the stage.

Those songs were to me what "Seems like You're Ready" was to Diamond in the Players Club.

FORTY-EIGHT

April 2007

University of Toledo
Toledo, Ohio

Sahara

I MET WITH AN ACADEMIC ADVISOR TO DISCUSS MY PROGress and my experiences with the university; a program initiated and implemented for the first-year students.

I was doing extremely well academically. 3.5 GPA…

At this appointment, the advisor advised me to consider other career paths, to imply that a career in writing is not always as promising as some would hope.

Although his words were realistic they cut too deep.

I became discouraged with being a writer. I couldn't think of anything else I wanted to do or be. I had never thought of a "Plan B". Heck, I never had a Plan A.

I was torn. I hadn't yet found who I was and I didn't know what I wanted to be. But what was definite was that I knew who and what I didn't want to become.

I had seen enough examples of "Do as I say, not as I do" but not any examples leading the way.

I planned to complete the semester and do some serious brainstorming over the summer break about my life and goals.

FORTY-NINE

May 2007

University of Toledo

Toledo, Ohio

Nina

I DIDN'T THINK I WOULD SEE THE DAY THAT I WOULD MISS home. Cleveland wasn't Beverly Hills but it was home. I couldn't find a corn beef sandwich or polish boy anywhere!

Five months in a dorm was a complete 360 from living in our own apartment.

Sahara had packed up and uprooted us with practically nothing. We took with us to Toledo only what could fit in our car. All our other belongings were given away for a little of nothing.

And it was all in vain! We would more than likely be coming back to Cleveland to stay. That advisor humbled her perfectionist, over achiever, know it all and never satisfied ass!

But to be clear, I did not have a problem with college. I had a problem with society pushing it on everyone as to say its everyone's One Way ticket to automatic success.

There are multimillionaires without college degrees. And there are individuals with baccalaureate degrees waiting tables at Applebee's. Degrees to me are like cars; depending on what you have and its type, people determine who you are and how much money you have.

There are many instances, however, that degrees are essential. Surely, I wouldn't want a surgeon performing surgery on me without the correct credentials.

I would want to be positive he was in fact a doctor trained and certified in surgery and not someone pretending to be a doctor with a piece a paper from a Cracker Jack Box.

I will never hold Sahara back from college if that's what she truly wanted but I don't want her to go in naively thinking she would be entitled to the "American Dream" simply because she would eventually be a college graduate.

FIFTY

July 2007

Cuyahoga Community College

Cleveland, Ohio

Sahara

IT HAD BEEN NEARLY A YEAR SINCE I SEEN MY BEST FRIENDS and play sister. And a few months since I had seen Rich.

Tashia and I had grown slightly distant since she became a mother of two and had a live-in fiancé.

Kia was home from Florida permanently. She partied her freshman year and was placed on academic probation. She would have had to pay for college out of pocket if she wanted to stay in school at Florida A&M. And that wasn't a practical possibility.

Tiffany was still Tiffany but those twins slowed her down a lot.

Rich had come to see me twice in Toledo but he merely came around when he was bored with his monthly fling. He hardly answered my calls, so I stopped calling and waited for him to call me.

Kia and I had agreed to meet at Tri C (Cuyahoga Community College) to take the nursing entrance exam. I had decided to let the idea of becoming an author rest; I was not going to return to Toledo.

Cleveland houses four of the top nationally recognized hospitals; University Hospitals, Veteran's Affairs, Metro Health Hospital and Cleveland Clinic.

Clevelanders who were either uncertain about their future and or wanted to earn a good secure living… became nurses. So, nursing it was for her and I.

We formerly had experienced in the field as nursing assistants. Therefore, it wasn't so farfetched for the two of us to switch our majors to nursing.

We both were successful with the entrance exam and was eligible to apply to their nursing program upon completion of prerequisite requirements.

I slept at night at Tiffany's place or with Kia at her mom's house until I could figure some things out.

FIFTY-ONE

July 2007

Cuyahoga Community College

Cleveland, Ohio

Aniya

WHEN I WAS COMING UP THERE WERE HARDLY ANY chocolate females to identify with.

My childhood friends and I would call the phone chat line, Cleveland Raven and set up double dates when we were bored.

The first question everyone would want to know is "What you look like"? Most would exaggerate and some people would blatantly lie. Like Yvette Wilson did as her character Rita in Friday. Call her Miss Jackson if you nasty!

Lies she told!!!

I on the other hand would always tell guys I favored Meelah of the 90s R&B group 702. I knew we didn't look alike but she was the best choice considering having limited options.

Sitting in the college's café dozing off, I heard a man's voice ask:

"Is this seat taken?" He pulled out the chair next to me.

"No," I answered. I studied his face. He looked familiar but I knew he wasn't an old fling. I could account for every man I laid with.

"I haven't seen you around lately," He added.

"Around?"

"Yeah, you don't remember me?" he finally took a seat beside me.

"Yeah I remember you," I lied attempting to avoid the guessing games.

"Sweet as Candy," He smiled. "I know you're a popular lady and you see a hundred men a day."

Mr. 200 singles! Nina searched high and low for him that night! I thought to myself.

"I remember. How are you? Thanks for the love handsome."

"I'm cool. I'm done with classes for the day. Would you mind having lunch with me if you're free?" Mr. 200 singles offered.

"Do I look like a girl who says no to a meal," I joked.

We hung out for an hour in the cafe, laughing, eating pizza and discussing everything but **sex**! *A first time for everything!*

FIFTY-TWO

August 2007

Cuyahoga Community College

Cleveland, Ohio

Sahara

IT HAPPENED AGAIN FOR THE UMPTEENTH TIME. I KNEW this person well but I didn't know how I knew him. And instead of embarrassing myself I kept quiet and played along.

And the great thing is that *they* hadn't messed it up for me yet!

"Good morning," he reached out for a hug.

"Good morning," I smiled. We hugged briefly.

"You want to eat here or somewhere else?" Mitch asked.

"Here is fine," I replied.

Mitch and I could sit and talked for hours. I liked him a lot. I didn't know our story but it was nice to enjoy his company for the moment.

I loved to pick folks' brains and play games like 20 questions.

I ran down the rules and the game logistics and I let him start.

"Number 1, what's your favorite food," he asked?

"Seafood but especially crab legs. How about you?"

"Banana Pudding."

"Number 1, what's your favorite movie," I asked?

"Paid in Full, Boys in the Hood, Scarface, Godfather and ..."

"Which Godfather," I interrupted?

"All of them," He added. "and Menace to Society. How about you?"

"Man what we will be here all darn day! Ok but just off the top of my head. My favorite all-time favorite is Imitation of life. The 1950 version, Straight tear jerker. Deep! But I have a lot of dramas. But ummmm, let me see: God father II, Men of Honor, Sister Act II, It's a Wonderful Life, Crash, American History X, Seven Pounds. My romance pick is Love and Basketball and comedy, Friday after Next, Liar Liar and ... ok that's enough! You get the point. I love movies!" I laughed because I knew I could list ten more movies effortlessly. "Your turn."

"Number 2, what's your favorite book," he asked.

"Oh man! I guess you really don't want to get rid of me today," I chuckled. "Flyy Girl, Tears of a Tiger, Dope Fiend, True to the Game- all of three of them before you ask, and I can't forget The Coldest Winter Ever. And yours?"

"I can't believe that's it for you. I thought you really were going to keep going and going. But mine will be Rich Dad Poor Dad and the Coldest Winter Ever. Oh and Black Men magazine," He laughed!

"That's not a book, crazy!" I chuckled.

"It is to me," we both laughed.

"Number 2, what's your favorite TV show," I asked.

"The Wire and Law and Order. Number 3, what's your favorite position?"

"Oh crap, I knew it was coming!"

"What that mean," he paused. "Okay don't answer."

"Sixty-nine. You," I stated dryly not wanting my idea of fun to turn sexual.

"Okay forget it. You really didn't want to answer that. Never mind."

"I answered. Your turn."

"Doggy-style"

"How did I guess," I stated unenthusiastically. "Do you have any more perversion to get out of your system now so we can go on with my game," the brat in me took over!

"I said forget it, dag! Your turn," he exclaimed.

"Number 3, where do you see yourself in 5 years?"

"Happily married with kids and well off into my career, Respiratory Therapist." It was refreshing to speak to a man with a vision and even more so to hear him share dreams of a promising future/career other than sports and music. "You?"

"Finished with nursing school and releasing my first novel. And everything else is still undecided."

"Number 4, what's your favorite sport?"

"Well, I'm not really the sports type. But the only sport I kind of like to watch and understand is basketball."

"Number 4, what was your first CD," I asked. Curious about his taste in music.

"Reasonable Doubt, Miseducation of Lauren Hill and The Untouchable. You?"

"Tupac's Best Hits 2 Disc Album, Xscape- Traces of My Lipstick, Kelly Price- Soul of a Woman, Mary J- Share my World and R. Kelly-12 play."

Our game was interrupted. The college was closed for the evening. We hadn't noticed we were the last students left in the building.

FIFTY-THREE

September 2007

Hillside Condominiums

Cleveland, Ohio

Sahara

KIA AND I FOUND A PLACE. A TWO-BEDROOM APARTMENT. It wasn't much but it was ours. It fit perfectly into our plans and price range.

We planned to split every bill down the middle, work hard, budget and complete nursing school. We had a year of prerequisites to do and then we would be able to apply to the nursing program.

There was no better person to have as a roommate. Kia was financially responsible, trustworthy and dependable.

And we both could save our money.

Birds of a feather flock together

-AUTHOR UNKNOWN

FIFTY-FOUR

September 2007

Hillside Condominiums

Cleveland, Ohio

Aniya

MR. 200 SINGLES A.K.A. MITCH WAS THE FIRST GUY I MET to make me want to change!

A week after we met I tried seducing him and he denied me; telling me that I was drunk and he wanted to have me when I could remember.

He loved Sahara's mind but he loved my body more if someone had asked me.

Mitch was any woman's dream come true. The epitome of a good man. Perfect gentleman. High morale.

Raised in a two-parent household his entire life. A God-fearing man; loyal, caring, smart, funny and supportive. Great provider.

The guy who still opens car doors, hold hands and walks on the outside of the street.

But as far as I was concerned he was overqualified.

He was nothing I had seen before.

Kia had stayed out with her boyfriend for the day and I was home alone. It was time for some sex. All my past lovers were in the wind. Out of sight, out of mind. After being gone for 5 months my bench players had switch teams.

I needed a whole new line up ASAP. I wanted to call Rich but I knew he was off limits. Sahara was crazy about her some Rich.

And besides he was too darn arrogant for me. I was used to being chased not doing the chasing.

I couldn't resist calling Mitch to come over. It's a shame I had to spoil a good thing. But a girl had needs.

FIFTY-FIVE

September 2007

Sweet as Candy

Cleveland, Ohio

Nina

FUCK A MAN! GIVE ME THE MONEY! THAT IS UNLESS HE'S giving me cash or teaching me how to get it. It's not a thing better than money.

Whomever said money can't buy happiness was a damn lie. When I have bread I eat the shit I like to eat. I eat with the elite. Expensive table cloths, cloth napkins, waiters in arm distance to fill up my glass after drinking two sips of wine and/or water; and where there's no such thing as a meal or combo. Seafood market value and side dishes a la carte.

I can buy whatever the hell I want without looking at price tags or asking, "How much is this"?

I can sleep peacefully knowing every bill I own is paid. I can take off work when I'm restless and not worry about my rent being short because of it.

I can plan a girl's trip with the ladies and not think twice about it.

I do what I want when I want and don't have to answer to a soul.

And I would probably believe that lame shit about money not being everything if I was still naive. But having experienced hunger, the ghetto and utility disconnections, I knew otherwise.

Not to add, last week I walked into the dealership, traded in my hoopty and smacked a wad of cash on the desk and walked out with a brand-new fire engine red Dodge Charger. The second big purchase I made after only saving for a few months.

"You see I don't go by an alias because this is my life I don't know anything else and I don't want to know anything else. I like to have sex, get money, get high, take a trick up top (a phrase used to describe exploitation of another individual's resources) and party. I started fucking at eleven. When I was sixteen, I slept with my mother's boyfriend, Mike (Mike was ten years younger than her mother and 6 years older than her). He didn't coerce me. I plotted it all. One night my moms went to work 11-7 as she usually did and I gave him a shot of Jose and it was all she wrote. I had his ass eating out the palm of my hand and I loved it. He was giving me everything I wanted and some. It was great until he really started loving me. He got my first place and wanted us to be together. The excitement was gone. It was no longer fun because we weren't sneaking around and creeping anymore. I had to move another sucka in to get rid of his ass. I'm the hoe yo momma warn you about and most broads fear. I'll smile in your face and be screwing yo man on the low." Alexis shared with me after I had walked in the bathroom on her wiping blood and cocaine dust from her nose.

I was back to work at Sweet's. It was like I had never left.

Alexis was an open book and didn't hide her love of the girl. She could be scandalous and cut throat.

She had no remorse for her actions. She hung alone and she would come prepared with whatever she needed to in the event a wife, girlfriend or side piece had come to seek vengeance.

Alexis had been in numerous fights since I had known her; and most times Alexis would deliver her triumphant package as requested. I assumed she must have had plenty of practice or her known drug habit gave her incredible she-man powers to fight so well.

Alexis continued to vent…

"But you on the other hand, you different and all us hoes know that. You know who you are so why does it matter why you're here and what you're doing now. This too shall pass. If you gotta crawl around on this dirty ass stage, get naked, give a lap dance, lead them on, pretend like you go both ways, listen to their weak ass game or their sob stories about their bitch or life or play like you like their fat, corny, ugly or smelly breath ass then you got to do what you got to do to get up out of here."

I didn't respond. It was not a secret I hated being there most nights and sometimes my unenthusiastic persona could be mistaken for arrogance and superiority.

Drinking alcohol soothed me of humility, guilt and helped me open up.

I watched from a far Alexis continue to snort cocaine. She closed her eyes and enjoyed the ride. Her body swayed back and forth. And she giggled every few seconds for no apparent reason.

But what she failed to realize is that she wasn't much different than I. Minor difference was we worshipped two different masters. Her master was white, mine was green.

I had totally forgotten about my patron waiting on me at the bar. I wondered about what else could be bothering Alexis that she wasn't disclosing.

I couldn't imagine anyone just wanting to get high just for the heck of it. I believed that there was something unbearable for that individual to be going through to resort to drug use.

I had a hard time understanding how folks could be so oblivious to their environment. What would make an individual think that what has happened to others that came before them committing the same acts would result in different outcomes?

Driving by the streets of the heart of the city was testimony. One couldn't help but notice the abandoned buildings and houses destroyed by drug infestation. Drug substances so potent that everything it touches is a subsequent to its demise.

I was almost certain for an individual to have been nonchalant of drug affects then it must have been for a good reason.

I walked back to the bar to return to the visit with one of my faithful clients. I enjoyed sitting with him and just talking.

He loved to listen to me talk about Sahara's dreams and aspirations. I didn't have any of my own. Becoming wealthy was my only end game.

We would have drinks and he would tip me simply for keeping him good company. Depending on how generous he felt, he would give me anywhere between $100-$300, 2-3 nights a week.

I loved it; I didn't have to grind on him, be phony or be fondled and I still made my money.

But my mind wandered thinking about Alexis, a much younger Violet.

FIFTY-SIX

January 2008

Downtown Flats

Cleveland, Ohio

Aniya

A NEW YEAR, A NEW LIFE. I WANTED SOMETHING NEW. Someone new. Our birthday was awesome! And I wanted the party to continue.

Mitch invited me out for the night. He picked me up at home and we headed down to the West Bank of the Flats.

We were having a great time when I noticed Sahara's former coworker, Zaria dancing on the dance floor. She was being flirtatious and dancing with two guys.

She would go from one to the other and back to the other. She was feeling both men up. I was turned on.

I signaled for Mitch to watch too. *I bet watching her have sex with Mitch would be more erotic!*

"Hey, I have someone for you to meet. She's kinky, she's cute, bisexual, a registered nurse and loaded with cash," I don't know why I mentioned money but I assumed he would be more willing if he knew she was above average.

"What you're telling me that for" He asked.

"Go get her!" I nudged.

"Nah girl. You drunk," He exclaimed! Mitch walked back to the bar and closed his tab. He was ready to leave.

FIFTY-SEVEN

The next day

Sahara

I ROLLED OVER WITH A MASSIVE HANGOVER. MITCH WAS being the kind, caring man he always was. Two tablets of Tylenol, a full glass of ginger ale and a bag of Salt and Vinegar chips was lying on my nightstand. My hangover concoction.

Being in college, studying and spending time with him made me forget about Rich, whom I hadn't heard from in weeks.

I was taking two courses, Anatomy and Physiology II and Intro to Psychology, before I would start the program in the fall.

I couldn't remember our night but I knew we had to have had fun because I didn't tie my hair up.

It had gotten to a point that I didn't have to write letters or draw the date on myself. I waited for the phone to ring or to come face to face with my acquaintances, friends or loved ones to get the update. I had begun to accept things as they were. I was different. And if my alter ego or egos hadn't committed a crime then there was room for us all to live in harmony.

"You acted like a different person last night. This character was different than the Sahara I know. You weren't even Nina (he put his fingers up replicating quotation marks). You tried to get me to talk to your co-worker. I think you had too much to drink," Mitch stated lying beside me.

"I did what," I asked. Trying to give myself time to formulate a response. I had no idea what he was talking about. *It happened again! What did I do?*

"You heard me" He exclaimed.

"That's crazy. Yeah, I must've been drunk! Well was she at least cute? Was her butt fatter than mine," I joked, trying to lighten the mood.

"Hell nah, she was sitting on flats," he laughed. "She was cute and all but you know you're all I need".

I blushed!

"I'm ok! I'm not all that," I grinned.

"Shiddd," He laughed.

FIFTY-EIGHT

March 2008

Hillside Condominiums

Cleveland, Ohio

Sahara

THE POPULAR QUOTE IN THE ANIMANIACS' CARTOON WAS stuck in my head. Character Pinky asked Brain, "What are we going to do today Brain?"

Brain would repeatedly reply, "Same thing we do every day, Pinky. Try to take over the world! "

It felt like the ambitious outgoing determined part of me had disintegrated. I used to want to take over the world and make a difference; mentor kids and provide a safe haven.

I wasn't living, I was existing.

Kia was gone a lot over to her boyfriend's, at school or working.

I looked around at our small rented two-bedroom apartment and wondered what difference was I making. I had done nothing of great significance.

I did not own one thing of true value. I had some materials and labels. Half of which I didn't really want but I thought I wanted. I had four top designers bags a Gucci, two Louis Vuitton and a Prada. I had about 25 affordable brand named purses like Aldo's, Coach, Guess and Nichole Lee.

I had shoes galore; some cheap but cute, many average priced like Jessica Simpsons, Steve Maddens and BCBG and a few disgustingly expensive pairs. Of the ridiculously priced shoes were a pair of Christian Louboutin pumps which were too narrow and torcher to walk in. No amount of boast was worth the pain. They stayed in their box on the shelf for display.

I had a couple pair of 2 K diamond studded earrings; a Movado watch; two heart tag choker Tiffany necklaces engraved with my initials, with the matching bracelets; a Pandora bracelet and a ton of Aldo's high end costume jewelry.

My wardrobe came along way from my high school days of Wet Seal, Rainbow, Marshalls and Charlotte Russe; accessorized with mall kiosk's jewelry and name plate belts.

I had $1659.42 in my checking account; $810 in my savings account; and $334 in cash. My bills and rent paid up.

I had the latest year car. But I felt empty and worthless.

I had a man in my bed, I hardly knew and who hardly knew me. But somehow our chemistry connected and voilà. He was my Tommy and I was his Kesha.

Rich and I had been dating on and off for years but had never formulated a conversation of substance. Our relationship was centered around sex.

I kind of felt I held a special place in his heart too. Rich would tell me constantly how pretty I was. He loved my natural state minus the weave, the make up, the hazel brown contact lenses and the false eye lashes.

He would often say, " I chose you because I'm different. All these young dudes are ignorant all they talk about is red/yellow bones. Like half their moms and sisters aren't dark skinned. If they truly loved and honored their mothers they ass would be singing a different song. My momma, my granny and aunts are all dark. And I love theeee hell out of them and I think they're the most beautiful women I know. But don't get me wrong I like red/ yellow women too. Hell, I like all women but I love my black ass beauties most," He chuckled.

I would roll my eyes not certain whether or not he had given me a backhanded compliment.

"Your skin is smooth and even, milk chocolate delight, not a pimple, not a blemish or crater on your face. You don't need no fucking makeup. Your hair is soft, thick, long and naturally wavy. Your eyes are commanding and genuine. You don't need them damn contacts! Your smile mesmerizing, inviting and contagious. If only you saw in you what I see in you. You the truth!" He added.

But I begged the differ. This day especially. I had drunk more Grey Goose doubles than I could tolerate and manage. I was consumed with sadness and misery.

Rich called me out the blue and asked to meet me at home. Intoxicatingly horny, I wasted no time pulling at Rich trousers in the stairwell of my apartment complex.

By the time, we reached my door his pants were at his knees and his greatest accessory was standing at attention. My extra-large extroverted nipples were on beam. My panties were damp at the very sight of my sexy lover.

I was eager to taste every inch of him. We reached the apartment and entered just enough to close the door. I tore off his wife beater; kissing, licking and gently nibbling at his Adam's apple, chin and shoulder blades.

I licked down the center line of his chest and six pack to the elastic waistband of his Ralph Lauren boxers. I could smell his pre-ejaculate or precum which increased my arousal.

I pushed him back to allow him to rest on the door. Kneeling and handless, I let the untamed beast out its cage with my mouth synchronously while rubbing his defined abs with my left hand and his left thigh with my right hand. A trick I knew all too well.

In a matter of seconds, Rich was near the point of climax. But I didn't want to be short changed. I raised to my feet and French kissed him as we stumbled over ourselves to the bedroom.

I undressed what was left of him. And he undressed me. He loved to suck my breast. His lips were so soft that I would have to fight back my orgasm in efforts to endure penile penetration.

Rich kissed down to my belly button then flipping me over on my stomach. He smacked my ass, propped my knees and pushed down on the top center of my back (doggy style).

He licked and kissed my clitoris until I begged for him to stop. Fragile and limp, Rich scooted my small framed 150-pound body to the edge of the bed where he stood near. Same position. He ripped inside of me full throttle. Twenty minutes of deep thrusts, grunts and moans filled the room. Rich was sprawled out on top of me in the same state as I, fragile and limp.

My euphoria wore off and I lifted Rich's sleeping body from mine. I intended to do a quick clean off at the sink but instead I laid my bare body in the cold waterless bath tub.

I thought back to the time I had mutilated myself. But this time I wanted to do something more permanent. I couldn't escape my thoughts. I hated my life and the woman I had become.

I was my happiest when I was intoxicated, climaxing and pay day. Which all were short lived spurts of satisfaction.

Looking at my reflection in the mirror I was no better or different than anyone else I tried to set myself apart from.

I wasn't a prostitute but I, ***she*** was a stripper. I wasn't a drug addict but I, ***she*** was a nympho. I wasn't homeless but I wasn't a home owner. I wasn't broke but I wasn't financial secured. I didn't think I was ugly but I didn't think I measured up to society's standard of gorgeous. I was a high-school graduate but I also was a college dropout. I wasn't a teen mom but I could've easily had been if I hadn't had an abortion. I was doing better than my mother but not as good as my father was doing at my age. I had lost my way and had no way of correcting it.

I glanced to my chest and saw my 14K gold cross and necklace glistening. I had never taken it off in ten years since it was first placed on my neck by mother for Christmas. Violet wore a cross around her neck and a rosary in her purse all the time. She believed that they kept her safe on her many nights of being at the wrong place at the wrong times. She would always say, "God protects fools and babies."

I could no longer stand the sight of that cross hanging from my neck. I don't know whether I disliked it because I felt like a hypocrite who no longer believed or because it was a gift from my mother. Either or it had to go. I took it off and folded it in tissue and placed it gently in the medicine cabinet.

I wasn't sure whether I believed in a "God" anymore.

I thought about everything I had gone through; all my loved ones who abandoned me.

I reached for the Tylenol in the medicine cabinet. I grabbed a handful of pills and gulp them down. If I had to guess I consumed three times the acetaminophen maximum daily dosage of 3,000 mg.

I drank some tap water from my palm to rinse it down. I took a peep in the bedroom at Rich and wondered if he would give two fucks if I was dead or not. And I quickly assumed that he wouldn't have cared whether I was dead or alive.

I gently kissed his freshly tapered nape and went back to the bathroom. I drifted off to sleep to allow nature to run its course.

FIFTY-NINE

Twenty – forty

minutes later

IT WAS A SCENE FROM PULP FICTION. INSTEAD OF BEING AN accidental heroine OD it was a Tylenol suicide OD. Rich came to the bathroom for his nightly ritual to urinate. And his foggy vision caught a glimpse of a hand hanging from the bath tub.

He pulled back the shower curtain and there Sahara laid naked, perspiring and unconscious. He panicked. He checked her wrist. They were free of cuts. He looked for blood. No splatter. "I would've heard a gunshot," he thought.

Then it dawned on him. He had two guns under the pillow. He ran in the room and knew he had to ditch the guns if he was going to have to call the ambulance because the police would be right behind them.

He couldn't chance leaving Sahara any longer to run to the car. He looked out the window. And luckily it was a bush just below her 3rd floor apartment. He tossed the guns out the window and made sure they fell right where he wanted them.

He ran back to the bathroom. He didn't know shit about medicine but he seen many paramedics in the hood try to revive his boys after they had been shot. He knew she wasn't dead he still seen her chest moving.

Rich lifted her out the tub to the bathroom floor when he noticed the sliding glass doors to the medicine cabinet cracked open. He opened the door and found Tylenol, floss, toothpaste, a ball of tissue, One a Day Woman vitamins, a contact case container and a Cover Girl Mascara.

"She took this fucking Tylenol," he guessed.

He held off on CPR and thought if he could get her to vomit, she maybe cool. He stuck his finger so far down her throat that he felt her tonsils.

Sahara dry heaved the first two attempts. She eventually let out a huge emesis. Rich repeatedly induced vomiting until her stomach was empty.

She slowly came to. Sahara looked around as if she were dreaming. She couldn't believe her eyes. It wasn't her time once again.

Rich lifted her up in his arms and cradled her like baby despite the smelly vomit she was covered in. He didn't flinch or speak. He just stared into her eyes. Sahara couldn't bear the idea of being pitied, she shamefully stared away at the floor.

He placed her in the tub and turned on the shower. She felt sick and drowsy. He grabbed her a bottle of water from the fridge; stepped in the tub and laid on the side of her.

Sahara took small sips until it was gone. As the cool water hit their faces and body, he thought about the events leading up to that moment. He wanted to know why she wanted to die. He wanted to know who hurt her. He wanted to know how long she's been hurting. He wanted to know who all knew about it. He felt helpless not knowing if he could fix her. He assumed that this maybe the one thing that money couldn't solve. Rich wrapped his arms around her and decided to ask her all his questions another day. Sahara softly wept!

To whom much is given
much is required

LUKE 12:48

SIXTY

Summer 2001

Warrensville Hts, Ohio

Sahara

DEAR DIARY,

Today was a rough day. Rougher than before. I can't stand the sight of my own face anymore. I just wanted to show someone how bad I hurt.

I took the razor down from my ponytail and wonder how I could hurt myself without killing myself. I started cutting. It's weird how something so painful could feel so good. It was something about the warm blood running down my arm to the floor that gave me satisfaction.

Unintentionally, I cut once too deep. I could see my muscle. I immediately got scared. Praying I hadn't damaged my arm. I started twisting my wrist and lifting imaginary weights to ensure it was still functioning properly. This made the blood ooze more. I grabbed a shirt from my drawer and held pressure to the sight.

After about 10 minutes, the bleeding stopped. It felt great to be back in control. I released some anger and frustration and now I was okay. I have no idea how the cut would heal. But I needed a reminder of tonight. I took the pink cami I had used to stop my bleeding and I soaked up the blood from the tile floor before disinfecting the area.

I placed the cami in a freezer Ziploc bag and I set back in silence for a moment. I set still processing what had just happen. And I couldn't believe it. I couldn't believe things had got so bad. I was supposed to be the chosen one. I was supposed to be the fortunate child. I was supposed to have it all. But in reality I am just as messed up as everyone else. I fucking hate my life!

SIXTY-ONE

May 2008

Hillside Condominiums

Cleveland, Ohio

Sahara

I HADN'T HEARD FROM RICH SINCE MY BREAKDOWN. I assumed he was getting the furthest away from me, the psycho, as he could get. Despite everything that was going on I had managed to pass both my classes with flying colors.

Kia and I would be starting the nursing program in August.

Mitch and I had gone to the Kem concert to celebrate my acceptance into the program. He made every effort to make me smile but sadly it was never enough.

I set watching his nose flare in and out, his chest rise and fall and him peaceful sleep next to my side. He slept like a baby without a care, regret or guilt in the world. I didn't deserve him. He was too good to me. He was too good for me and he had the slightest clue. What about me was he attracted to? I was mentally screwed up. I was broken. Could he fix me? Was he up for the challenge at hand? I couldn't possibly mess up this good man's life. I wasn't worth his time and love.

He was a client turned friend, turned friend with benefits, turned lover; A line I hoped we had never crossed. But living with two other women kind of made having boundaries impractical. He had made his way around to us all. Just like many of my other relationships I had hoped I had gotten another chance for them just to meet ME. But fact of the matter was I was who I was and THEY were a part of me. Damage was done! Hurt people hurt people!

SIXTY-TWO

June 2008

Justice Center

Cleveland, Ohio

State of Ohio

Vs.

Richard Williams

and Khalil Rodrigues

TWO MEN SAT PATIENTLY WAITING FOR THEIR DAY IN court. Both men were dressed to kill and present with their separate counsel. Dressed in tailor suits and perfectly groomed "to a tee". If I hadn't known any better, I would have thought it was some sort of mix up and the guys before me where groomsmen and not county inmates on trial.

Thanks to the internet, I learned of his whereabouts.

I set on a row with about eight other women all waiting to witness the fate of the defendant(s). There were women of all shapes, colors, and sizes. No two women looked alike so it was hard to see who was with who. But one thing that was for certain we all sat to the right of the courtroom behind the defense. It was just a matter of time before we would be acquainted to our fellow bench-mate.

"All rise," court room bailiff gave the room orders to stand. "Judge Alicia Russo residing."

The prosecutor and attorneys approached the bench. They spoke law jargon and shuffled around documents. Rattled off a few numbers and said exhibit this and exhibit that and then it was time for the first witness.

"The state calls it first witness, Shavon Leah Gaines-Dorsey"

Shavon Leah Gaines-Dorsey enters the courtroom with a perplexed expression. Not sure if it were nerves or fear. She looked vaguely familiar but then again it seemed as if I knew everyone I came across from somewhere.

"Please raise your right hand. Repeat after me. I do solemnly swear to tell the whole truth and nothing but the truth so help me God"

She exhaled deeply and repeated what she was asked to. She fidgets around in the seat. First, smoothing out her skirt and then pulling and tugging at her size too small top. Prosecutor approaches the stand.

"Hello, would you please tell the court what occurred on the evening of September 21, 2006"

"I called Mr. Rodrigues over to my home after my husband had gone out of town," she stated.

"So, Mr. Rodrigues is your or was your boyfriend." asked the prosecutor?

"Yes, he was. We had been dating for about one month. My husband and I weren't getting along at the time," Shavon confessed.

"Is Mr. Rodrigues present today?"

The witness pointed to Mr. Khalil Rodrigues, tall Hispanic male, one of the two co-defendants on trial.

"Let the record note that Mrs. Gaines-Dorsey has positively identified Khalil Rodrigues."

"What happen when Mr. Rodrigues arrived at your home?"

"We started having sex in the kitchen and then we went up to the bedroom. While having sex, I heard a noise coming from downstairs."

"And you two continued on?"

"Yes, I thought it may have been my cat or something we had bumped in the kitchen that fell down."

"What happen next?"

"Five minutes or so I heard a man say: Let me get some of that!"

"Where was the voice coming from?"

"There with us, inside the bedroom. I thought that it was my husband."

"Did you know this person?"

"No I don't believe so. He was a white guy dressed in all black and wearing a ski mask."

"Where was Mr. Rodrigues at this time?"

"He was standing beside me, in between the nightstand and my bed."

"What happen next?"

"I jumped across the bed to grab my husband gun but it was gone. Mr. Rodrigues then pulled me by my hair and dragged me back onto the bed."

"What was the other man doing?"

"He had pulled out a gun and pointed it at me. And he asks again if he could hit that"

"What was Mr. Rodrigues doing at this time?"

"He threw my jeans at me and told the guy: Not on my watch. That's not what we're here for. That's when I knew that they knew one another."

"Objection your honor," Khalil's defense attorney interrupted.

"Yes," Judge Russo exclaimed. Khalil's attorney shuffled through papers.

"I'm waiting," the judge grew inpatient.

"Just a second your honor," he stated broadcasting his inexperience, immaturity and impromptu skills.

"That's not how it works Mr. Kopeck. You need to know what your objection is before you disrupt the witness testimony. Go ahead Mrs. Dorsey."

"What happen next?" the prosecutor resumed.

"Mr. Rodrigues told me to get dress and we all went back downstairs to the kitchen. When we got to the kitchen two other men were sitting at my table."

"Did you know these two men?"

"No. But both men were black. One light skin and the other dark brown. They too were wearing ski masks."

"Where was Mr. Rodrigues at this time?"

"Mr. Rodrigues was near the door and looking out the shades."

"Did the other men say or do anything else?"

"Mr. Williams asked where we kept our money...."

"Objection your honor. Speculation!" Rich's defense attorney objected.

"Sustained," the judge ruled. "The jury will disregard the last remark."

"A moment to speak with the witness your honor?" The prosecutor asked the judge. The judge nodded in agreeance. The prosecutor approached the stand, covering the mic and whispered to the witness.

"Rephrase the question your honor! What happen after you entered the kitchen and seen the two unknown men wearing ski masks at your table?"

"The man with lighter skin asked where we kept our money?" Mrs. Gaines-Dorsey re-answered the question. "I told them all that we didn't have any money there."

"What happen next?"

"Mr. Rodrigues then told me that I should tell them where the money was because he didn't want them to hurt me. The white guy stood behind me and rubbed the barrel tip across the front of my jeans on my vagina. And he kissed my neck."

"What did you do then?"

"I was afraid of getting raped so I showed them where we hid our money in the wall. They took all our savings. And the light skin black guy duct taped my mouth shut and my hands together. He told me not to move until they were gone."

"Did anything else happen before they left your home with your savings?"

"The light skin guy walked me in the broom closet and gave me a message for my husband: tell your punk ass man to think twice next time he threatens one of mine! And he closed the door."

"Defense's witness your honor," the prosecutor concluded.

Rich defense attorney stood and approached the stand. "Have you ever seen my client, Mr. Williams before?"

"I don't know. Maybe."

"Have you or have you not seen my client's face before?"

"No, I haven't seen him before."

"Why were you hiding money at your home?"

"My husband doesn't like banks," she professed.

"I bet because he's a criminal!"

"Objection your honor!" the prosecutor interrupted.

"Sustained. Knock it off Mr. McKinney! Jury disregard the defense last remark."

"How much money was taken from your home Mrs." Mr. McKinney continued.

"$22,700"

"What kind of work do you and your husband do?"

"I am a licensed nail technician and I volunteer for the woman's shelter. My husband owns his own beauty and barber shop and he is a kids' football coach"

"How do we know you weren't the mastermind behind it all. I mean you did state that you and your husband weren't exactly the best of friends."

"Every marriage has problems. I love my husband and my husband loves me. I would never steal from him. Anything I want he gives me."

"Apparently not," the defense chuckled.

"Objection!" the prosecutor cried out.

"Sorry your honor. Jury disregard!" Mr. McKinney grinned.

"Last warning," the judge declared. She gave the defense attorney a cold stare.

"Would you state your husband's full name for the record?"

"Charles Scott Dorsey," the witness answered.

"Defense will like to enter BCI report for Charles Dorsey into evidence," Rich's lawyer stated.

"Objection your honor, relevance?" the prosecutor yelled." The witness or her husband are not on trial here."

"Ma'am I am simply presenting facts and verifying the integrity of the witness. The witness' husband is a 3 times convicted felon of Drug Distribution. I only want to establish credibility," Mr. McKinney pleaded.

"Sustained. Your treading on thin ice Mr. McKinney. Be careful." the judge cautioned.

"Thank you, your honor," Mr. McKinney stated gratefully.

"Moving on, in the police report you stated that the man who bonded your hands and feet, who you are alleging to be my client, was a couple inches taller than you. Will you state your height for the record?" Mr. McKinney asked.

"Five foot six," Mrs. Gaines-Dorsey replied.

"Would the record note that my client is six foot three inches. The defense rest."

The trial was paused for recess. And I kept thinking about the witness testimony. Could Rich had really done this? Was he capable of invading someone's home, taking their money, tying them up and leaving them trapped in a closet?

The prosecution had yet to prove guilt but I still felt uneasy about the whole thing. I had had enough for the day. I didn't want to hear anymore. I went home at recess.

SIXTY-THREE

June 2008

Dave's Bar and Grill

Cleveland, Ohio

Nina

I COULDN'T STAND THE SIGHT OF HER MOPING AROUND another second about that good for nothing dude. *Wish she would have listened to me years ago. I need a drink,* I thought to myself.

Why she loved that ole slick talking high yellow street dude was beyond me? I of all people knew she (we) deserved better. I guess I could have been a little more understanding and nicer since he did save our life.

I thought about Manny. It had been sometime since we last spoke.

We all were overdue a vacation. I called his cellular phone to learn that the number had been changed and or disconnected.

I drove down the street from our home to have a drink.

"Double of Grey Goose straight up with a can of Red Bull please!" I asked the bartender. She went on to prepare my drink.

I tried not to eavesdrop as I attempted to collect my own thoughts but I couldn't help but hear the bartender's conversation as she spoke loud enough for the entire bar to hear her and the male patron conversing.

"The city will sleep better now that the jack boys are off the streets."

"They finally got stung because they had got sloppy."

"I can't believe they hit Scotty for 300 Gs."

"Don't nobody have no work now."

"All the bottom dealers struggling."

"Even my money been slow."

I looked down at my phone pretending to be occupied and not listening when she returned with my drink. I guzzled down my drink before she could walk ten paces and threw $15 on the bar counter and ran for the door to my car.

Was the "Jack boys" she referred to Rich and Khalil? What was the chance that Rich robbed Scotty? As a matter fact ol' girl, the witness did look familiar.

That was Shay! That was Scotty's wife. I can't believe it took me so long to put it together. ***Charles Scott Dorsey,*** *well I be damn!!*

I flipped thru the pages of my planner to find the approximate date I paid off Daddy's headstone which would tell me the time of the Reese and Scotty ordeal. And it matched the time frame of the witness testimony. She testified that she hadn't long met Khalil and the other guy with him stated that he was also there to seek payback.

The entire car ride I drove in silence, analyzing and interpreting every detail of Shay's testimony.

I had learned the truth but will Sahara believe it! And how could I tell her?

SIXTY-FOUR

June 2008

Hillside Condominiums

Cleveland, Ohio

Sahara

"HELLO THIS IS GLOBAL TELL LINK……." THE AUTOmated voice spoke through the receiver. Rich was attempting to call me. I dialed 1 to accept the call.

"What's up chocolate?" he said surprisingly cheerful.

"Hey babe," I replied.

"I didn't see you in court today," he stated.

"I had to work," I lied.

"Oh okay. Well I just called to see how you were doing. My lawyer is on top of everything. Things are looking good. They ain't got nothing on me. But the judge doesn't like my lawyer at all. They have history."

"Well I pray that things work out for you. Can you call me back later? I'm still working." I didn't want to talk. I needed time to think about me and my life.

"OK. I'll call you after chow!" We hung up.

I didn't trust him anymore. Between the women at the trial and his charges, I didn't know who I was dealing with. I knew that we weren't never officially a couple and I knew he dealt with other women but I didn't know to what degree or how many women it was. I had a hunch that all those women at trial were there for him. And then hearing the witness' testimony, I was confused. I had been sleeping with a menace. I probably wouldn't have felt so bad if the victim was a man but how could he have done that to a woman.

I wanted to confront him but it wasn't the time or place. I needed answers. Who were those women? And was he guilty?

He called later in the day as asked. But I ignored his call.

Sahara

All the evidence against Rich was circumstantial. Khalil's next door neighbor testified that Khalil and Rich were best friends and that she had seen them both together after the incident. Which I had never seen or heard of Khalil before in the 2 years of knowing Rich. She also testified that she seen Khalil carrying a black duffle bag shortly after the incident allegedly occurred. Forensic scientist stated that a partial finger print found at the scene was discovered on the kitchen table where Rich was allegedly sitting; and it was a 30% match. And lastly, Rich fit the description of a light skin African American male noted in the police report. But his attorney argued the height discrepancy, the sketchy print and the hearsay made by the neighbor.

After five days of deliberation, a verdict was returned guilty on all counts of aggravated burglary, aggravated robbery and aggravated kidnapping. Rich and Khalil were sentenced to 30 years with the possibility of parole. Alleged suspects 3 and 4 were never identified.

My heart poured out for Rich, even if he were guilty. I couldn't imagine a 29 years old individual having to spend the rest of their life behind bars. His nine years old son would grow up fatherless. Rich will never marry. He will never get a second chance to do right. He would be 59 years old if he survived prison; and everything and everyone he knew would have changed.

SIXTY-FIVE

August 2008

Cuyahoga Community College

Cleveland, Ohio

Sahara

TWO WEEKS INTO THE PROGRAM AND THINGS WERE already intense. It was encouraged that we formed study groups to be successful in the course. I had made friends with a few of my classmates in my study group. The study group seemed to be beneficial, I earned a 90% on my first quiz.

Kia and I had been separated. I was in the day classes and she was in the evening classes. But she was doing well also.

One hour of death by power point, we were given a 15-minute break.

I used my break to use the ladies room. Ten seconds later the bathroom stall door flung open and my classmate stood in front of me licking her lips.

"Damn you don't know how much I been thinking about you," Yasmine expressed.

"Excuse me," I replied baffled.

"I can't believe you can prance around as if nothing happened," She stated.

"I don't know what you're talking about Yasmine. Excuse me," I asked nicely trying to exit the stall.

"You never came by my house? I never tasted you?" she stepped aside for me to walk by her.

"Look Yasmine, you're a nice girl and all and I don't want any problems. I'm trying to pass this class, get through this program and be a nurse. I don't know what you're talking about and I want to forget this conversation occurred."

I washed my hands and left Yasmine standing alone in the restroom.

Things had gone too far. I was livid.

If only I could get a hold to a chastity belt. It was one thing for ***her*** to sleep with men but now women! *I can't take it. What's next an orgy party?*

One hour later

Aniya

I stayed quiet long enough. I let everyone have their chance. But I'm the realest there is. I'm that little voice every woman has but is too afraid to act on. Who don't like a good time and a good screw?

Too many people care about what other people think. Hell, I love what I love. If the H.B.I.C. prefers to self-indulge, over exert and attempt to plan and control every detail of her life and later hate herself for not measuring up than that's her prerogative.

If Lady Paper Chaser b.k.a Nina would rather get paid for baring skin and trying to get rich in a game that so many have failed at well then that's her prerogative.

But don't fault me for seeking what I love.

I dare anyone try to judge me. I do what most only dream of doing if no one were to find out.

I love sex and oral sex especially but ain't no damn orgy party going down. I run the damn show. I want to be the only one in control. Won't nobody be rough housing and taking advantage of me. I like a tight vagina and I want to keep it that way. *Who the hell do she think I am?*

It was one damn time. And I had been on a drought.

Just because Sahara would rather find the perfect guy (that doesn't exist), be faithful and get married and have kids, don't make her better than me. She dumb as hell and delusional.

All men are dogs and want one thing. She can't get mad at me for beating them at their own game!

At least I'm not getting lied to, cheated on, degraded and left feeling insecure, unattractive and worthless.

She can keep hoping and wishing for a miracle fairy tale; while I run shit and have my way!

SIXTY-SIX

Labor Day 2008

Red Lobster

Beachwood, Ohio

Sahara

MITCH CALLED ME OUT TO HAVE DINNER AND DRINKS with him. We met there, sat and ate and talked like the good ole days.

We ordered four rounds of Long Island Ice Tea cocktails and was working on a fifth when we were made aware that the restaurant was near closing.

Unsteady and wobbling, I was indeed under the influence. Mitch offered to drive me home but I refused. I was confident I could make it home safely.

I decided to drive the streets route instead of the freeway which I normally traveled.

Ten minutes into the drive, I regretted deciding to drive the streets. I attempted to fight through the combination of exhaustion and alcohol.

I had not had a good night sleep in weeks I had been studying nonstop.

I let down the windows to feel the cool night's breeze. I blasted the radio; all efforts made to stay awake.

I would talk to myself. "You got it! Ten more minutes and so for…"

Every few seconds, I would catch myself nodding off and one mile closer to home. And I would check the clock, the road and note that I was close.

I prayed if I could stay awake for a few more minutes I would be home and safe in my bed.

And then I drifted off to sleep once more but this time I was too slow catching myself.

A green Ford Explorer was 15 feet in front of me at the stop light.

Oh shit! Tires screeched… BAM!!

And with a blink of an eye my 2008 Charger was totaled. Easy come easy go!!

As quickly as Nina had put the 5K deposit down to pull off Ganley's lot with our best car to date with only two hundred miles at the time of purchase, it was gone!

The police were on the scene in minutes.

The other driver, a middle-aged Asian male assured I was okay and drove away, before police could request a statement. He too was intoxicated.

Thankfully, hardly any damages were done to his car.

I walked away with a single scratch from what should have left me immobile and debilitated. The entire front end of my car was concaved.

The officer on scene requested a field sobriety test, which I consented to. During the tandem walk, the test was halted by the officer's commander.

His commander simply said, "Let her go". Ironically, his commander had once been one of Nina's loyal clients.

I was allowed to leave the scene with a warning. I had been saved from possible death and serious injury, possible manslaughter, assault, regret, prison and at the very least a career killer.

I reached for my neck and realized my cross was gone but someone somewhere was still present and watching over me.

SIXTY-SEVEN

September 2008

Cuyahoga Community College

Cleveland, Ohio

Sahara

I WAS SITTING IN MY NURSING FUNDAMENTAL COURSE LIStening to the instructor cover the Respiratory lecture. The instructor begins to play an audio video of adventitious breath sounds. As a class, we were responsible for identifying the abnormal sounds as crackles, rhonchi or wheezes and listing their possible diagnoses and other associated signs and symptoms.

And in walks the program director, she called the last names of three students. All women looked nervously around at each other to ponder what their similarities could be. One by one the director met with each woman to seal their fate.

The rest of us tried to regain attention but set distracted wondering what was happening with our classmates.

After class, we learned all three women had failed their BCI background check. The women prior offenses were: drug possession, petty theft and check fraud.

Yasmine was one of the three women. Subsequently they all were removed from the program.

It was upsetting to see my classmates attempting to get their lives together only to have their past had come to haunt their future.

Yet I was relieved that I had been spared from the humility I faced seeing Yasmine every class day.

I felt blessed to have made it out. I couldn't help but imagine if certain circumstances had occurred differently against my favor then I would have been walking in her/their shoes.

Like the time, I got into a scuffle with a couple of DTW "down the way" girls and ***she*** razor slit the face of one of my assailants. I felt horrible afterwards but what could I have done with 3 against 1.

Or not that long ago, when I dodged the DUI offense. Or the many times the young naive me wanted to be a "ride or die" chick to a knuckle head that I don't talk to anymore for whatever reason and who probably don't even remember my name.

We wouldn't ask why a rose that grew from the concrete for having damaged petals, in turn, we would all celebrate its tenacity, we would all love its will to reach the sun, well, we are the roses, this is the concrete and these are my damaged petals, don't ask me why, thank god, and ask me how

-TUPAC SHAKUR

SIXTY-EIGHT

Sahara

IT WAS SOMETHING ABOUT THAT MAN THAT I COULDN'T shake. I was still in lust. And I couldn't turn my back on him after all he had done for me.

He didn't judge me when he had every reason to. He cared for me when I didn't care for myself. I owed him for that if nothing else.

"Lorain Correctional...." The lady deputy answered.

"Hi, I would like to schedule a visit," I stated.

"Inmate Number?"

"651122340"

"Richard Williams?" she asked.

"Yes, ma'am"

"For what date?"

"This Saturday morning," I replied.

"Saturday 12/6 morning," she confirmed.

"Yes!"

"What's your name?"

"Sahara Ramal."

"You're all set. Reservation number: K- Kilo, S- Sierra, 2136 C-Charlie, T- Tango.

"KS2136CT, got it. Thanks!"

SIXTY-NINE

Nina

I WENT TO WORK AT SWEET'S FOR THE NIGHT AND SEEN A new name on the roster. A new name being on the roster wasn't as alarming as the name itself.

I looked all around the club for this mysterious woman with the familiar name. And then I finally found her coming out of V.I.P.

She looked like she had aged since the last time I had seen her. She was still pretty but her glow was gone.

Her eyes wore dark bags and her spirit had lost its bubble.

"What are you doing here, Yasmine?"

"Same reason you're here, Sahara!" she replied.

"My name is Nina. And you don't belong here."

"And you do?"

"This life chose me, not the other way around. And besides it temporary."

"Well I have to do what I have to do since I can no longer be a nurse," She exclaimed!

"But this isn't the answer. This game will eat you up and spit you out. Yeah you the shit today. Your body banging and you're a pretty girl. But what happens when they use you up and you're not the fresh tender on the block anymore? What extreme will you take to regain that momentum and attention again that you once owned?" I tilted my head in the direction of the dancer to our right who was practically giving her client a hand job right in front of us.

"Or will you then start doing drugs?" I pointed to Alexis on stage.

"Or will you start cutting and altering your body?" I glanced in the north direction, two seats ahead at Tokyo.

"Will you start crossing boundaries you promised you wouldn't just to earn another $1000? What's your out? Or do you think you can strip forever?" I pointed to Pebbles.

Yasmine gulp down the double shot of Remy Martin she had been holding. She walked over three seats from where we were standing and asked a patron did he want a dance. He replied, yes.

She stared back at me as if I was the enemy and I was attempting to deceive her for my own personal gain. I scold myself for intruding. This was totally out of my character. That was the sort of thing Sahara did but not me. I was foolish for thinking I could tell a grown ass woman anything about her life and her decisions.

I promised from that day forward that I wouldn't pry again. Hell, I wouldn't even acknowledge her. I would go back to the life I knew before she existed; come get my money, mind my business and go home.

SEVENTY

Sahara

RICH CAME WALKING IN THE VISITING ROOM WITH HIS navy-blue jumpsuit. He was still as attractive as he was in street clothes.

I felt like I was happier to see him than he was to see me. I was cheesing from ear to ear.

He still knew how to make my skin shiver, my heart race, my mouth water and my tummy rumble just by smiling.

I fantasized about the days and nights we competed for orgasms. *Who could make who cum the fastest!*

My legs began to tremble. I clinched my knees tight to stop my clitoris from pulsating.

I stood from the table to hug him.

We hugged so long that the correctional officer yelled out to him. "Break it up, Williams. That's enough!"

I enjoyed every minute of our three hours visit until it was time to go.

He reassured me that he and his brothers were working on his appeal.

We said our goodbyes and I exited the visiting room in a single file line with the other visitors.

Once we reached the jail lobby, I noticed the afternoon visitors were being processed.

Coincidentally or divine intervention, I recognized one of the females waiting in the lobby from Rich's trial.

I stalled around in despair of refuting my assumption.

As I predicted, the unknown female was identified as Ms. Ashley Simmons and she was there to visit Richard Williams.

And that was enough for me to wipe my hands of him. I shared him when he was free and I refused to share him incarcerated.

I was finally done. It was time to move on. *I deserved better!*

SEVENTY-ONE

Nina

YOUNG ZAY WAS PERFORMING AT SWEET'S. I WAS THRILLED to be working. I knew I would probably make about one thousand dollars easy. When Young Zay would come through the club he showed the girls love.

I had an outfit made special for the night. I figured it took money to make money. I had no problem dropping two fifty on an outfit when I was making it right back and some.

I ran to the dressing room to be the first girl on the floor when he entered the building. It's true what they say, the early bird gets the worm.

I was front and centered at 10 'o clock sharp.

About thirty minutes later, I seen a camera and video crew setting up. I was puzzled. I ran back to the dressing room to ask Destiny what was going on.

She informed me that Young Zay and several other local rappers and singers were performing and we all would be in their music video.

I was pissed instantly.

I wanted the money but I couldn't hurt Sahara. I went to find the club's owner to clarify the detailed arrangements for the night.

"Andre, what's going on," I asked?

"You ready to make this paper, Nina," he replied.

"Yeah I was. But what s up with the cameras and shit," I asked.

"Don't tell me you're shy, baby," he laughed.

"Not shy at all. But I don't need my face on no footage that may end up in everyone hands."

"Well I don't know what to tell you baby. Most would love this type of exposure," he stated.

"Well, I'm not most. I'm me. And I don't want to be on camera," I demanded!

"That's your choice. But the camera will be rolling at twelve. You can stay or you can leave."

"You absolutely right," I replied.

I headed to the dressing room, got dressed and hugged Missy goodbye.

I left that night and never looked back. I knew my days there were coming to end but I couldn't predict that and not that soon.

I am the greatest, I said that even before I knew I was

-MUHAMMAD ALI

SEVENTY-TWO

Sahara

MY PHONE WAS TURNED OFF FOR A WEEK. I HAD NOTHing to say to Rich or anyone else. I had nine missed voice messages; Two from Tiffany, two from Violet, two from Rich and three from Mitch.

I went out to the mall for some retail therapy when I ran into Mitch. Mitch was standing in line for a gourmet pretzel when I noticed a woman standing beside him.

They both were laughing and smiling uncontrollably, the kind of emotions new couples share in the honeymoon stage. He held on to her hand while they stood in line.

At first sight, I wanted to confront them. I didn't like the idea of fighting over a guy but for him I was willing to make an exception.

I knew I could have had him and take him back but it wouldn't have been fair to him.

His happiness was warranted. I didn't have a right to be selfish. I walked by them and pretended not to have known them.

SEVENTY-THREE

Sahara

I WENT TO WORK AT SUNSHINE RETIREMENT COMMUNITY for the weekend. My beloved Mrs. Francis' death anniversary was near.

Mrs. Francis had expired early the next morning after I had consoled her relative in the restroom. She had fought a good fight and was cherished by many. She passed away surrounded by a gang of friends and family.

When I reached the break room, I noticed her family had provided the staff with refreshments, flowers and a thank you card just like the years prior.

I had this deep urge to make amends and be at peace. I began to write.

Dear mama,

I was angry. I was disappointed. You were supposed to be the world to me. You were supposed to protect me. You were supposed to be there. And you weren't. But what I'm most disappointed with is your lack of effort. You not only gave up on me but most disturbingly you gave up on you.

I am sorry that you had no woman figure in your life to resemble. I am sorry bad things happen to you as a child. I am sorry you grew up poor. I am sorry no one told you to be all you can be. I am sorry your family support hasn't been so supportive of your dreams and your future. I am sorry that you didn't know better to do better. I am sorry for every tear you cried and every hurt you ever felt. If I could I would take all your pain away.

I would tell you that you're the prettiest woman I've ever seen so that you wouldn't need to hear it from any man. I would tell you how smart you are and assist you with your homework when you're struggling with something. I would listen and console you whenever you needed it. I would provide all your necessities so that you wouldn't have to do "God knows what" for it.

I would make it so that you didn't want for anything in the world. I would teach you the things a woman should teach a girl. I would teach you how to cross your legs. I would treat you to a girls' day of pampering. We will get our hair and nails done and go shopping.

I would teach you what fork is used for salad and what spoon is used for soup. I would teach you the proper way to clean and cook. I would be there the first day when you started your menstrual cycle to explain the do's and don'ts. I would talk to you about your precious temple.

I would warn you about drugs and the root to all evil, better known as money. I would give you the mother I wish you had; So that maybe you would had been the mother I wished you were to me.

But that's a life of "if I would've, should've, could've". It is what it is. And I have learned to accept things as they are. I now understand that there is no blueprint for parenting. And you did what you felt was best for me. I also realized that our creator may have given me to you to help you. Maybe I was sent here to love, protect, inspire and assist you to change. There had to be a reason why you are still here and Jason and Daddy weren't.

Sometimes events don't occur in the politically correct chronological order of sequence as we're used to. We all assume that a mother should raise the child. But in our case, maybe the child is supposed to raise the mother. You never missed a birthday or holiday, even if all you did was call or send a card.

Twenty plus years ago, you let me invade your space. You put your life at risk so I can have mine. Somewhere in your thought process you determined I was worth the trouble.

Your life wasn't a fairytale and neither has mine been. But if we never were to speak after today, I want you to know that I love you. You were not the mother that I needed you to be and that's okay. Could you have done better? Yes. But hey I'm not going to dwell on it. Cause you know what? You could've also been a hell of a lot worse. So, mommy I love you. And I forgive you!

Love Sahara

Dear daddy,

You left me way before I could blossom and I was still so very fragile, young, naive and oblivious. Your death was the second most turning point in my life. Nothing would have prepared me for your death.

I hated you for leaving. I felt betrayed, cheated and robbed. You left a void no one has yet or will ever fill. I listen to Luther Vandross, "Dance with my Father Again" and can't help but think of us. You were my hero and my everything. I wish you would have warned me that that day would come.

You were the first parent of anyone my age that I had known to die. I had no clue this could have and would have happened to me. I thought mommy would go before you.

You once carried a butchered cow over your shoulder. You stood up to toughest dudes on Saint Clair and no one messed with you. You were worshipped and adored through the streets of Cleveland. No one could mention St. Clair without mentioning you, your store, your food and/or bar.

Econo Marts, home of the coldest beer in town and the best corn beef sandwich; overnights you spent rotating the beers in the cooler from the back to the front to have the perfect blend of ice and chill. If the beer stayed in the freezer a moment too long it would burst and if it was taken out a moment too soon it wouldn't measure up. You had coined in on the recipe for delivering what many of your customers crazed.

The love you gave seasoning your corn beef and making sure it was extra tender to out beat your competitors was priceless.

Daddy you were the MAN. You were too strong to let anything take you out. Cancer! Shit..... that didn't stand a chance to the man I called daddy. So, I thought!

You were full of wisdom and will power. There wasn't one time you let me down. If you said you were coming you came. On occasion, you may have been late but you were there. If you said you would do it, you did it!

I kept your coat to remember your smell. I try to write down all the memories we shared so I won't forget. I want to remember you when I'm 50 just as I did at 15. One of my deepest fears is forgetting any part of you.

I love you to the moon and back. They don't make men or fathers like you anymore. And I am blessed to have had you the time that I did.

I used to question that sometimes. Is it better to have "loved and lost or to have never loved at all?" And now I can say with 100% certainty, I would give anything to have you here now but knowing and loving you for as little as I did is worth more to me than anything else in this world.

I now understand that if you could have fought it, you would have. God was ready for his angel. I love you and I'm sorry for being bitter and unapologetic all these years!

Till we meet again my first love,
Love Sahara

Dear ***all of me,***

I want to tell you that I love you unconditionally. And I no longer am ashamed of you. I created you as some sort of coping/defense mechanism. I embrace you. I forgive you for the past, presence and future.

I have come to accept that no one is perfect. We are who we are! You were my protection, my defense and my strength. We may not see eye to eye on everything; but you both made me who I am and I am eternally grateful.

Yours Truly,
Sahara

It's one of the greatest gifts you can give yourself, to forgive. Forgive everybody

- MAYA ANGELOU

SEVENTY-FOUR

Sahara

MY HEART WAS DOING CART WHEELS AND MY ADRENAline was flowing continuous. My hands were shaking and sweating.

The day had finally come, fifty-three weeks of pure dedication and resilience. Kia and I were college graduates and soon to be licensed nurses.

I had did it!

I was next in formation to be called. The college's Dean of Nursing announced my name and I could hear my mother screaming to the top of her lungs from the balcony.

Tears of joy ran down my cheeks.

I was no longer just a crack baby, a troubled teen, a problem child, a fast girl, a mentally unstable being, a lost cause or a stripper.

In fact, I am a believer and a fighter. I am my father's child! We shared the same undeniable wit!

I shook the hands of the Dean and my professors. I exited the stage and blew a kiss to the sky.

Daddy, I got next…

God bless the child who has its own

- BILLIE HOLIDAY